# PIRATES!

# PIRATES!

*Classic Tales of Treasure, Mayhem, and*
*High Seas Skullduggery*

EDITED BY
TOM MCCARTHY

LYONS PRESS
Guilford, Connecticut
*An imprint of Globe Pequot Press*

*For Maggie and Britta: Smooth sailing.*

Lyons Press is an imprint of Globe Pequot Press.

Project editor: Lauren Brancato
Layout: Melissa Evarts

Library of Congress Cataloging-in-Publication Data is available on file.

ISBN 978-0-7627-9454-6

Printed in the United States of America

10 9 8 7 6 5 4 3 2 1

# CONTENTS

# INTRODUCTION

The reality of piracy, even today, is much different and more ominous than the romantic and enticing stories in this collection.

But viewed through the fog and distance of history, pirates are a downright—should I say it?—lovably gnarly group of miscreants. And pirate stories have long entertained and enthralled readers, generation after generation.

The pirate, as they would say in the good old days when all of these stories were written, is an undeniably redoubtable figure—both in real life and in literature. The pirate is a cad, a ne'er-do-well, a scoundrel bent on mayhem. He is unkempt, drunken, leering, unshaven, and irrepressible.

He is not bound by the rigid strictures of society, and by his very nature and his often outrageous activities, he is a bane to common everyday social mores.

In other words, he's free to do whatever he wants, whenever he wants to.

Let's face it, there is a certain amount of universal sympathy for the pirate—a bit of maybe not-so-hidden identification with the brigand in all of us who wants to get out.

*Oh, you decided you no longer need the report I stayed up all night to finish because you're taking the day off?*

*Wait—the oil change is going to cost $1,650 because you found a blown head gasket?*

*The dance recital is four hours long and we have to sit through the entire thing?*

*Aaaarrrgh!*

*To the plank, all of you.*

Part of the general allure of pirates is that these characters embody the romance of the sea. The sea's very openness means independence. And that magic is what readers have looked for over the years. That is why these stories will draw you in.

If human beings were scoundrels and savages on land, they were doubly so at sea. And as sailors made their way across the oceans and discovered everything there was to discover, pirates preyed on them. And as the world became more civilized, its righteousness could not eradicate the germ of piracy. Growing worldwide commerce sparked piracy; it made it inevitable. Piracy went hand-in-hand with the Age of Discovery. It made for hardier sailors, great, adventurous, romping stories, and colorful characters, real and fictional.

The fact remains, and will always remain: In the lore of the sea, the pirate is far and away an almost picturesque figure. And the more real or imagined his career the higher the degree of interest he inspires.

And the more writing he inhabits and inspires.

This collection continues the tradition.

# The Pirate's Code

## *Philip Gosse*

The conditions of life on a pirate ship appear to have been much the same as on all vessels. On procuring a craft by stealing or by mutiny of the crew, the first thing the pirates had to do was to elect a commander. This was done by vote among the crew members, who elected whoever they considered the most daring among them, and the best navigator. The next officer chosen was the quartermaster. Once the captain and quartermaster were elected, the former could appoint any junior officers he chose. The shares in any plunder the pirates took was divided according to the rank of each pirate. The crew was then searched for a pirate who could write, and, when found, this scholar would be taken down to the great cabin, given pen, ink, and paper, and after the articles governing order on the ship had been discussed and decided upon, they were written down, to be signed by each member of the crew. As an example, the articles drawn up by the crew of Captain John Phillips on board the *Revenge* are given below in full:

### 1.

*Every man shall obey civil Command; the Captain shall have one full Share and a half in all Prizes; the Master, Carpenter, Boatswain and Gunner shall have one Share and a quarter.*

### 2.

*If any Man shall offer to run away, or keep any Secret from the Company, he shall be marroon'd with one Bottle of Powder, one Bottle of Water, one small Arm, and Shot.*

### 3.

*If any Man shall steal any Thing in the Company, or game, to the value of a Piece of Eight, he shall be Marroon'd or shot.*

### 4.

*If at any Time we should meet another Marrooner (that is, Pyrate,) that Man that shall sign his Articles without the Consent of our Company, shall suffer such Punishment as the Captain and Company shall think fit.*

### 5.

*That Man that shall strike another whilst these Articles are in force, shall receive Moses's Law (that is 40 Stripes lacking one) on the bare Back.*

### 6.

*That Man that shall snap his Arms, or smoak Tobacco in the Hold, without a cap to his Pipe, or carry a Candle lighted without a Lanthorn, shall suffer the same Punishment as in the former Article.*

7.

*That Man that shall not keep his Arms clean, fit for an Engagement, or neglect his Business, shall be cut off from his Share, and suffer such other Punishment as the Captain and the Company shall think fit.*

8.

*If any Man shall lose a Joint in time of an Engagement, shall have 400 Pieces of Eight; if a limb, 800.*

9.

*If at any time you meet with a prudent Woman, that Man that offers to meddle with her, without her Consent, shall suffer present Death.*

# Blackbeard in Virginia

## *Howard Pyle*

The governor's proclamation against the pirates was issued upon the eleventh day of November. It was read in the churches the Sunday following and was posted upon the doors of all the government custom offices in lower Virginia. Lieutenant Maynard, in the boats that Colonel Parker had already fitted out to go against the pirates, set sail upon the seventeenth of the month for Ocracoke. Five days later the battle was fought.

Blackbeard's sloop was lying inside of Ocracoke Inlet among the shoals and sand bars when he first heard of Governor Spottiswood's proclamation.

There had been a storm, and a good many vessels had run into the inlet for shelter. Blackbeard knew nearly all of the captains of these vessels, and it was from them that he first heard of the proclamation. He had gone aboard one of the vessels—a coaster from Boston. The wind was still blowing pretty hard from the southeast. There were maybe a dozen vessels lying within the inlet at that time, and the captain of one of them was paying the Boston skipper a visit when Blackbeard came aboard. The two captains had been talking together. They instantly ceased when the pirate came down into the cabin, but he had heard enough of their conversation to catch its drift.

"Why d'ye stop?" he said.

"I heard what you said. Well, what then? D'ye think I mind it at all?

"Spottiswood is going to send his bullies down here after me. That's what you were saying. Well, what then? You don't think I'm afraid of his bullies, do you?"

"Why, no, Captain, I didn't say you was afraid," said the visiting captain.

"And what right has he got to send down here against me in North Carolina, I should like to ask you?"

"He's got none at all," said the Boston captain, soothingly. "Won't you take a taste of Hollands, Captain?"

"He's no more right to come blustering down here into Governor Eden's province than I have to come aboard of your schooner here, Tom Burley, and to carry off two or three kegs of this prime Hollands for my own drinking."

Captain Burley—the Boston man—laughed a loud, forced laugh. "Why, Captain," he said, "As for two or three kegs of Hollands, you won't find that aboard. But if you'd like to have a keg of it for your own drinking, I'll send it to you and be glad enough to do so for old acquaintance' sake."

"But I tell you what 'tis, Captain," said the visiting skipper to Blackbeard, "they're determined and set against you this time. I tell you, Captain, Governor Spottiswood hath issued a hot proclamation against you, and 't hath been read out in all the churches. I myself saw it posted in Yorktown upon the customhouse door and read it there myself. The governor offers one hundred pounds for you, and fifty pounds for your officers, and twenty pounds each for your men."

"Well, then," said Blackbeard, holding up his glass, "here, I wish 'em good luck, and when they get their hundred pounds for me they'll be in a poor way to spend it. As for the Hollands," said he, turning to Captain Burley, "I know what you've got aboard here and what you haven't. D'ye suppose ye can blind me? Very well, you send over two kegs, and I'll let you go without search." The two captains were very silent. "As for that Lieutenant Maynard you're all talking about," said Blackbeard, "why, I know him very well. He was the one who was so busy with the pirates down Madagascar way. I believe you'd all like to see him blow me out of the water, but he can't do it. There's nobody in His Majesty's service I'd rather meet than Lieutenant Maynard. I'd teach him pretty briskly that North Carolina isn't Madagascar."

On the evening of the twenty-second the two vessels under command of Lieutenant Maynard came into the mouth of Ocracoke Inlet and there dropped anchor. Meantime the weather had cleared, and all the vessels but one had gone from the inlet. The one vessel that remained was a New Yorker. It had been there over a night and a day, and the captain and Blackbeard had become very good friends.

The same night that Maynard came into the inlet a wedding was held on the shore. A number of men and women came up the beach in oxcarts and sledges; others had come in boats from more distant points and across the water. The captain of the New Yorker and Blackbeard went ashore together a little after dark.

The New Yorker had been aboard of the pirate's sloop for all the latter part of the afternoon, and he and Blackbeard had been drinking together in the cabin. The New York man was now a little tipsy, and he laughed and talked foolishly as he and Blackbeard were rowed ashore. The pirate sat grim and silent.

It was nearly dark when they stepped ashore on the beach. The New York captain stumbled and fell headlong, rolling over and over, and the crew of the boat burst out laughing.

The people had already begun to dance in an open shed fronting upon the shore. There were fires of pine knots in front of the building, lighting up the interior with a red glare. A negro was playing a fiddle somewhere inside, and the shed was filled with a crowd of grotesque dancing figures—men and women. Now and then they called with loud voices as they danced, and the squeaking of the fiddle sounded incessantly through the noise of outcries and the stamp and shuffling of feet.

Captain Teach and the New York captain stood looking on. The New York man had tilted himself against a post and stood there holding one arm around it, supporting himself. He waved the other hand foolishly in time to the music, now and then snapping his thumb and finger.

The young woman who had just been married approached the two. She had been dancing, and she was warm and red, her hair blowzed about her head. "Hi, Captain, won't you dance with me?" she said to Blackbeard.

Blackbeard stared at her. "Who be you?" he said.

She burst out laughing. "You look as if you'd eat a body," she cried.

Blackbeard's face gradually relaxed. "Why, to be sure, you're a brazen one, for all the world," he said. "Well, I'll dance with you, that I will. I'll dance the heart out of you."

He pushed forward, thrusting aside with his elbow the newly made husband. The man, who saw that Blackbeard had been drinking, burst out laughing, and the other men and women who had been standing around drew away, so that in a little while the floor was pretty well cleared. One could see the negro now; he sat on a barrel at the end of the room. He grinned with his white teeth and, without stopping in his fiddling, scraped his bow harshly across the strings, and then instantly changed the tune to a lively jig. Blackbeard jumped up into the air and clapped his heels together, giving, as he did so, a sharp, short yell. Then he began instantly dancing grotesquely and violently.

The woman danced opposite to him, this way and that, with her knuckles on her hips. Everybody burst out laughing at Blackbeard's grotesque antics. They laughed again and again, clapping their hands, and the negro scraped away on his fiddle like fury. The woman's hair came tumbling down her back. She tucked it back, laughing and panting, and the sweat ran down her face. She danced and danced. At last she burst out laughing and stopped, panting. Blackbeard again jumped up in the air and clapped his heels. Again he yelled, and as he did so, he struck his heels upon the floor and spun around. Once more everybody burst out laughing, clapping their hands, and the fiddling stopped.

Nearby was a shanty or cabin where they were selling spirits, and by and by Blackbeard went there with the New York captain, and presently they began drinking again.

"Hi, Captain!" called one of the men, "Maynard's out yonder in the inlet. Jack Bishop's just come across from t'other side. He says Mr. Maynard hailed him and asked for a pilot to fetch him in."

"Well, here's luck to him, and he can't come in quick enough for me!" cried out Blackbeard in his hoarse, husky voice.

"Well, Captain," called a voice, "will ye fight him to-morrow?"

"Aye," shouted the pirate, "if he can get in to me, I'll try to give 'em what they seek, and all they want of it into the bargain. As for a pilot, I tell ye what 'tis—if any man hereabouts goes out there to pilot that villain in 'twill be the worst day's work he ever did in all of his life. 'Twon't be fit for him to live in these parts of America if I am living here at the same time." There was a burst of laughter.

"Give us a toast, Captain! Give us something to drink to! Aye, Captain, a toast! A toast!" A half dozen voices were calling out at the same time.

"Well," cried out the pirate captain, "here's to a good, hot fight to-morrow, and the best dog on top! 'Twill be, Bang! bang!—this way!"

He began pulling a pistol out of his pocket, but it stuck in the lining, and he struggled and tugged at it. The men ducked and scrambled away from before him, and then the next moment he had the pistol out of his pocket. He swung it around and around. There was perfect silence. Suddenly there was a flash and a stunning report, and instantly a crash and tinkle of broken glass. One of the men cried out, and began picking and jerking at the back of his neck. "He's broken that bottle all down my neck," he called out.

"That's the way 'twill be," said Blackbeard.

"Lookee," said the owner of the place, "I won't serve out another drop if 'tis going to be like that. If there's any more trouble I'll blow out the lantern."

The sound of the squeaking and scraping of the fiddle and the shouts and the scuffling feet still came from the shed where the dancing was going on.

"Suppose you get your dose to-morrow, Captain," some one called out, "what then?"

"Why, if I do," said Blackbeard, "I get it, and that's all there is of it."

"Your wife'll be a rich widdy then, won't she?" cried one of the men; and there was a burst of laughter.

"Why," said the New York captain, "why, has a—a bloody p-pirate like you a wife then—a—like any honest man?"

"She'll be no richer than she is now," said Blackbeard.

"She knows where you've hid your money, anyways. Don't she, Captain?" called out a voice.

"The divil knows where I've hid my money," said Blackbeard, "and I know where I've hid it; and the longest liver of the twain will git it all. And that's all there is of it."

The gray of early day was beginning to show in the east when Blackbeard and the New York captain came down to the landing together. The New York captain swayed and toppled this way and that as he walked, now falling against Blackbeard, and now staggering away from him.

Early in the morning—perhaps eight o'clock—Lieutenant Maynard sent a boat from the schooner over to the settlement, which lay some four or five miles distant. A number of men stood lounging on the landing, watching the approach of the boat. The men rowed close up to the wharf, and there lay upon their oars, while the boatswain of the schooner, who was in command of the boat, stood up and asked if there was any man there who could pilot them over the shoals.

Nobody answered, but all stared stupidly at him. After a while one of the men at last took his pipe out of his mouth.

"There ben't any pilot here, master," said he; "we ben't pilots."

"Why, what a story you do tell!" roared the boatswain. "D'ye suppose I've never been down here before, not to know that every man about here knows the passes of the shoals?"

The fellow still held his pipe in his hand. He looked at another one of the men.

"Do you know the passes in over the shoals, Jem?" said he.

The man to whom he spoke was a young fellow with long, shaggy, sunburnt hair hanging over his eyes in an unkempt mass. He shook his head, grunting, "Na—I don't know naught about t' shoals."

"'Tis Lieutenant Maynard of His Majesty's navy in command of them vessels out there," said the boatswain. "He'll give any man five pound to pilot him in." The men on the wharf looked at one another, but still no one spoke, and the boatswain stood looking at them. He saw that they did not choose to answer him. "Why," he said, "I believe you've not got right wits—that's what I believe is the matter with you. Pull me up to the landing, men, and I'll go ashore and see if I can find anybody that's willing to make five pound for such a little bit of piloting as that."

After the boatswain had gone ashore the loungers still stood on the wharf, looking down into the boat, and began talking to one another for the men below to hear them.

"They're coming in," said one, "to blow poor Blackbeard out of the water."

"Aye," said another, "he's so peaceable, too, he is; he'll just lay still and let 'em blow and blow, he will."

"There's a young fellow there," said another of the men; "he don't look fit to die yet, he don't. Why, I wouldn't be in his place for a thousand pound."

"I do suppose Blackbeard's so afraid he don't know how to see," said the first speaker.

At last one of the men in the boat spoke up.

"Maybe he don't know how to see," said he, "but maybe we'll blow some daylight into him afore we get through with him."

Some more of the settlers had come out from the shore to the end of the wharf, and there was now quite a crowd gathering there, all looking at the men in the boat.

"What do them Virginny 'baccy-eaters do down here in Caroliny, anyway?" said one of the newcomers.

"They've got no call to be down here in North Caroliny waters."

"Maybe you can keep us away from coming, and maybe you can't," said a voice from the boat.

"Why," answered the man on the wharf, "we could keep you away easy enough, but you ben't worth the trouble, and that's the truth."

There was a heavy iron bolt lying near the edge of the landing. One of the men upon the wharf slyly thrust it out with the end of his foot. It hung for a moment and then fell into the boat below with a crash.

"What d'ye mean by that?" roared the man in charge of the boat. "What d'ye mean, ye villains? D'ye mean to stave a hole in us?"

"Why," said the man who had pushed it, "you saw 'twasn't done a purpose, didn't you?"

"Well, you try it again, and somebody'll get hurt," said the man in the boat, showing the butt end of his pistol.

The men on the wharf began laughing. Just then the boatswain came down from the settlement again, and out along the landing. The threatened turbulence quieted as he approached, and the crowd moved sullenly aside to let him pass. He did not bring any pilot with him, and he jumped down into the stern of the boat, saying, briefly, "Push off."

The crowd of loungers stood looking after them as they rowed away, and when the boat was some distance from the landing they burst out into a volley of derisive yells.

"The villains!" said the boatswain, "they are all in league together. They wouldn't even let me go up into the settlement to look for a pilot."

The lieutenant and his sailing master stood watching the boat as it approached.

"Couldn't you, then, get a pilot, Baldwin?" said Mr. Maynard, as the boatswain scrambled aboard.

"No, I couldn't, sir," said the man. "Either they're all banded together, or else they're all afraid of the villains. They wouldn't even let me go up into the settlement to find one."

"Well, then," said Mr. Maynard, "we'll make shift to work in as best we may by ourselves. 'Twill be high tide against one o'clock. We'll run in then with sail as far as we can, and then we'll send you ahead with the boat to sound for a pass, and we'll follow with the sweeps. You know the waters pretty well, you say."

"They were saying ashore that the villain hath forty men aboard," said the boatswain.

Lieutenant Maynard's force consisted of thirty-five men in the schooner and twenty-five men in the sloop. He carried neither cannons nor carronades, and neither of his vessels was very well fitted for the purpose for which they were designed. The schooner, which he himself commanded, offered almost no protection to the crew. The rail was not more than a foot high in the waist, and the men on the deck were almost entirely exposed. The rail of the sloop was perhaps a little higher, but it, too, was hardly better adapted for fighting. Indeed, the lieutenant depended more upon the moral force of official authority to overawe the pirates than upon any real force of arms or men. He never believed, until the very last moment, that the pirates would show any real fight. It is very possible that they might not have done so had they not thought that the lieutenant had actually no legal right supporting him in his attack upon them in North Carolina waters.

It was about noon when anchor was hoisted, and, with the schooner leading, both vessels ran slowly in before a light wind that had begun to blow toward midday. In each vessel a man stood in the bows, sounding continually with lead and line. As they slowly opened up the harbor within the inlet, they could see the pirate sloop lying about three miles away. There was a boat just putting off from it to the shore.

The lieutenant and his sailing master stood together on the roof of the cabin deckhouse. The sailing master held a glass to his eye.

"She carries a long gun, sir," he said, "and four carronades. She'll be hard to beat, sir, I do suppose, armed as we are with only light arms for close fighting."

The lieutenant laughed.

"Why, Brookes," he said, "you seem to think forever of these men showing fight. You don't know them as I know them. They have a deal of bluster and make a deal of noise, but when you seize them and hold them with a strong hand, there's naught of fight left in them. 'Tis like enough there'll not be so much as a musket fired to-day. I've had to do with 'em often enough before to know my gentlemen well by this time."

Nor, as was said, was it until the very last that the lieutenant could be brought to believe that the pirates had any stomach for a fight.

The two vessels had reached perhaps within a mile of the pirate sloop before they found the water too shallow to venture any farther with the sail. It was then that the boat was lowered as the lieutenant had planned, and the boatswain went ahead to sound, the two vessels, with their sails still hoisted but empty of wind, pulling in after with sweeps.

The pirate had also hoisted sail, but lay as though waiting for the approach of the schooner and the sloop.

The boat in which the boatswain was sounding had run in a considerable distance ahead of the two vessels, which were gradually creeping up with the sweeps until they had reached to within less than half a mile of the pirates—the boat with the boatswain maybe a quarter of a mile closer. Suddenly there was a puff of smoke from the pirate sloop, and then another and another, and the next moment there came the three reports of muskets up the wind.

"By zounds!" said the lieutenant. "I do believe they're firing on the boat!" And then he saw the boat turn and begin pulling toward them.

The boat with the boatswain aboard came rowing rapidly. Again there were three or four puffs of smoke and three or four subsequent reports from the distant vessel. Then, in a little while, the boat was alongside, and the boatswain came scrambling aboard.

"Never mind hoisting the boat," said the lieutenant; "we'll just take her in tow. Come aboard as quick as you can." Then, turning to the sailing master, "Well, Brookes, you'll have to do the best you can to get in over the shoals under half sail."

"But, sir," said the master, "we'll be sure to run aground."

"Very well, sir," said the lieutenant, "you heard my orders. If we run aground we run aground, and that's all there is of it."

"I sounded as far as maybe a little over a fathom," said the mate, "but the villains would let me go no nearer. I think I was in the channel, though. 'Tis more open inside, as I mind me of it. There's a kind of a hole there, and if we get in over the shoals just beyond where I was we'll be all right."

"Very well, then, you take the wheel, Baldwin," said the lieutenant, "and do the best you can for us."

Lieutenant Maynard stood looking out forward at the pirate vessel, which they were now steadily nearing under half sail. He could see that there were signs of bustle aboard and of men running around upon the deck. Then he walked aft and around the cabin. The sloop was some distance astern. It appeared to have run aground, and they were trying to push it off with the sweeps. The lieutenant looked down into the water over the stern, and saw that the schooner was already raising the mud in her wake. Then he went forward along the deck. His men were crouching down along by the low rail, and there was a tense quietness of expectation about them. The lieutenant looked them over as he passed them. "Johnson," he said, "do you take the lead and line and go forward and sound a bit." Then to the others: "Now, my men, the moment we run her aboard, you get aboard of her as quick as you can, do you understand? Don't wait for the sloop or think about her, but just see that the grappling irons are fast, and then get aboard. If any man offers to resist you, shoot him down. Are you ready, Mr. Cringle?"

"Aye, aye, sir," said the gunner.

"Very well, then, be ready, men; we'll be aboard 'em in a minute or two."

"There's less than a fathom of water here, sir," sang out Johnson from the bows. As he spoke there was a sudden soft jar and jerk, then the schooner was still. They were aground.

"Push her off to the lee there! Let go your sheets!" roared the boatswain from the wheel. "Push her off to the lee."

He spun the wheel around as he spoke. A half a dozen men sprang up, seized the sweeps, and plunged them into the water.

Others ran to help them, but the sweeps only sank into the mud without moving the schooner. The sails had fallen off and they were flapping and thumping and clapping in the wind. Others of the crew had scrambled to their feet and ran to help those at the sweeps. The lieutenant had walked quickly aft again. They were very close now to the pirate sloop, and suddenly some one hailed him from aboard of her. When he turned he saw that there was a man standing up on the rail of the pirate sloop, holding by the back stays.

"Who are you?" he called, from the distance, "and whence come you? What do you seek here? What d'ye mean, coming down on us this way?"

The lieutenant heard somebody say, "That's Blackbeard hisself." And he looked with great interest at the distant figure.

The pirate stood out boldly against the cloudy sky. Somebody seemed to speak to him from behind. He turned his head and then he turned round again.

"We're only peaceful merchantmen!" he called out. "What authority have you got to come down upon us this way? If you'll come aboard I'll show you my papers and that we're only peaceful merchantmen."

"The villains!" said the lieutenant to the master, who stood beside him. "They're peaceful merchantmen, are they! They look like peaceful merchantmen, with four carronades and a long gun aboard!" Then he called out across the water, "I'll come aboard with my schooner as soon as I can push her off here."

"If you undertake to come aboard of me," called the pirate, "I'll shoot into you. You've got no authority to board me, and I won't have you do it. If you undertake it 'twill be at your own risk, for I'll neither ask quarter of you nor give none."

"Very well," said the lieutenant, "if you choose to try that, you may do as you please; for I'm coming aboard of you as sure as heaven."

"Push off the bow there!" called the boatswain at the wheel. "Look alive! Why don't you push off the bow?"

"She's hard aground!" answered the gunner. "We can't budge her an inch."

"If they was to fire into us now," said the sailing master, "they'd smash us to pieces."

"They won't fire into us," said the lieutenant. "They won't dare to."

He jumped down from the cabin deckhouse as he spoke, and went forward to urge the men in pushing off the boat. It was already beginning to move.

At that moment the sailing master suddenly called out, "Mr. Maynard! Mr. Maynard! They're going to give us a broadside!"

Almost before the words were out of his mouth, before Lieutenant Maynard could turn, there came a loud and deafening crash, and then instantly another, and a third, and almost as instantly a crackling and rending of broken wood. There were clean yellow splinters flying everywhere. A man fell violently against the lieutenant, nearly overturning him, but he caught at the stays and so saved himself. For one tense moment he stood holding his breath. Then all about him arose a sudden outcry of groans and shouts and oaths. The man who had fallen against him was lying face down upon the deck. His thighs were quivering, and a pool of blood was spreading and running out from under him. There were other men down, all about the deck. Some were rising; some were trying to rise; some only moved.

There was a distant sound of yelling and cheering and shouting. It was from the pirate sloop. The pirates were rushing about upon her decks. They had pulled the cannon back, and, through the grunting sound of the groans about him, the lieutenant could distinctly hear the thud and punch of the rammers, and he knew they were going to shoot again.

The low rail afforded almost no shelter against such a broadside, and there was nothing for it but to order all hands below for the time being.

"Get below!" roared out the lieutenant. "All hands get below and lie snug for further orders!"

In obedience the men ran scrambling below into the hold, and in a little while the decks were nearly clear except for the three dead men and some three or four wounded. The boatswain, crouching down close to the wheel, and the lieutenant himself were the only others upon deck. Everywhere there were smears and sprinkles of blood.

"Where's Brookes?" the lieutenant called out.

"He's hurt in the arm, sir, and he's gone below," said the boatswain.

Thereupon the lieutenant himself walked over to the forecastle hatch, and, hailing the gunner, ordered him to get up another ladder, so that the men could be run up on deck if the pirates should undertake to come aboard. At that moment the boatswain at the wheel called out that the villains were going to shoot again, and the lieutenant, turning, saw the gunner aboard of the pirate sloop in the act of touching the iron to the touch-hole. He stooped down. There was another loud and deafening crash of cannon, one, two, three—four—the last two almost together—and almost instantly the boatswain called out, "'Tis the sloop, sir! Look at the sloop!"

The sloop had got afloat again, and had been coming up to the aid of the schooner, when the pirates fired their second broadside now at her. When the lieutenant looked at her she was quivering with the impact of the shot, and the next moment she began falling off to the wind, and he could see the wounded men rising and falling and struggling upon her decks.

At the same moment the boatswain called out that the enemy was coming aboard, and even as he spoke the pirate sloop came drifting out from the cloud of smoke that enveloped her, looming up larger and larger as she came down upon them. The lieutenant still crouched down under the rail, looking out at them. Suddenly, a little distance away, she came about, broadside on, and then drifted. She was close aboard now. Something came flying through the air—another and another. They were bottles. One of them broke with a crash upon the deck. The others rolled over to the farther rail. In each of them a quick-match was smoking. Almost instantly there was a flash and a terrific report, and the air was full of the whiz and singing of broken particles of glass and iron. There was another report, and then the whole air seemed full of gunpowder smoke.

"They're aboard of us!" shouted the boatswain, and even as he spoke the lieutenant roared out, "All hands to repel boarders!"

A second later there came the heavy, thumping bump of the vessels coming together.

Lieutenant Maynard, as he called out the order, ran forward through the smoke, snatching one of his pistols out of his pocket and the cutlass out of its sheath as he did so. Behind him the men were coming, swarming up from below. There was a sudden stunning report of a pistol, and then another and another, almost together. There was a groan and the fall of a heavy body, and then a figure came jumping over the rail, with two or three more directly following. The lieutenant was in the midst of the gunpowder smoke, when suddenly Blackbeard was before him.

The pirate captain had stripped himself naked to the waist. His shaggy black hair was falling over his eyes, and he looked like a demon fresh from the pit, with his frantic face. Almost with the blindness of instinct the lieutenant thrust out his pistol, firing it as he did so. The pirate staggered back: he was down— no; he was up again. He had a pistol in each hand; but there was a stream of blood running down his naked ribs. Suddenly, the mouth of a pistol was pointing straight at the lieutenant's head. He ducked instinctively, striking upward with his cutlass as he did so.

There was a stunning, deafening report almost in his ear. He struck again blindly with his cutlass. He saw the flash of a sword and flung up his guard almost instinctively, meeting the crash of the descending blade. Somebody shot from behind him, and at the same moment he saw some one else strike the pirate. Blackbeard staggered again, and this time there was a great gash upon his neck. Then one of Maynard's own men tumbled headlong upon him. He fell with the man, but almost instantly he had scrambled to his feet again, and as he did so he saw that the pirate sloop had drifted a little away from them, and that their grappling irons had evidently parted.

His hand was smarting as though struck with the lash of a whip. He looked around him; the pirate captain was nowhere to be seen—yes, there he was, lying by the rail. He raised himself upon his elbow, and the lieutenant saw that he was trying to point a pistol at him, with an arm that wavered and swayed blindly, the pistol nearly falling from his fingers. Suddenly his other elbow gave way and he fell down upon his face. He tried to raise himself—he fell down again. There was a report and a cloud of smoke, and when it cleared away Blackbeard had staggered up again. He was a terrible figure—his head nodding down upon his breast. Somebody shot again, and then the swaying figure toppled and fell. It lay still for a moment—then rolled over—then lay still again.

There was a loud splash of men jumping overboard, and then, almost instantly, the cry of "Quarter! quarter!" The lieutenant ran to the edge of the vessel. It was as he had thought: The grappling irons of the pirate sloop had parted, and it had drifted away. The few pirates who had been left aboard of the schooner had jumped overboard and were now holding up their hands.

"Quarter!" they cried. "Don't shoot!—quarter!" And the fight was over.

The lieutenant looked down at his hand, and then he saw, for the first time, that there was a great cutlass gash across the back of it, and that his arm and shirt sleeve were wet with blood. He went aft, holding the wrist of his wounded hand. The boatswain was still at the wheel. "By zounds!" said the lieutenant, with a nervous, quavering laugh, "I didn't know there was such fight in the villains."

His wounded and shattered sloop was again coming up toward him under sail, but the pirates had surrendered, and the fight was over.

# The Terrible Ladrones

## *Richard Glasspoole*

On the 17th of September, 1809, the Honorable Company's ship *Marquis of Ely* anchored under the Island of Sam Chow, in China, about twelve English miles from Macao, where I was ordered to proceed in one of our cutters to procure a pilot, and also to land the purser with the packet. I left the ship at 5 p.m. with seven men under my command, well armed. It blew a fresh gale from the northeast. We arrived at Macao at 9 p.m., where I delivered the packet to Mr. Roberts, and sent the men with the boat's sails to sleep under the Company's Factory, and left the boat in charge of one of the Compradore's men; during the night the gale increased. At half-past three in the morning I went to the beach, and found the boat on shore half-filled with water, in consequence of the man having left her. I called the people, and baled her out; found she was considerably damaged, and very leaky. At half-past 5 a.m., the ebb-tide making, we left Macao with vegetables for the ship.

One of the Compradore's men who spoke English went with us for the purpose of piloting the ship to Lintin, as the Mandarines, in consequence of a late disturbance at Macao, would not grant permission for regular pilots. I had every reason to expect the ship in the roads, as she was preparing to get under weigh when we left her; but on our rounding Cabaretta-Point, we saw her five or six miles to leeward, under weigh, standing on the starboard tack: it was then blowing fresh at northeast. Bore up, and stood towards her; when about a cable's length to windward of her, she tacked; we hauled our wind and stood after her. A hard squall then coming on, with a strong tide and heavy swell against us, we drifted fast to leeward, and the weather being hazy, we soon lost sight of the ship. Struck our masts, and endeavored to pull; finding our efforts useless, set a reefed foresail and mizzen, and stood towards a country-ship at anchor under the land to leeward of Cabaretta-Point. When within a quarter of a mile of her she weighed and made sail, leaving us in a very critical situation, having no anchor, and drifting bodily on the rocks to leeward. Struck the masts: after four or five hours hard pulling, succeeded in clearing them.

At this time not a ship in sight; the weather clearing up, we saw a ship to leeward, hull down, shipped our masts, and made sail towards her; she proved to be the Honorable Company's ship *Glatton*. We made signals to her with our handkerchiefs at the mast-head, she unfortunately took no notice of them, but tacked and stood from us. Our situation was now truly distressing, night closing fast, with a threatening appearance, blowing fresh, with hard rain and a heavy sea; our boat very leaky, without a compass, anchor or provisions, and drifting fast on a lee-shore, surrounded with dangerous rocks, and inhabited by the most barbarous pirates. I close-reefed my sails, and kept tack and tack 'till daylight, when we were happy to find we had drifted very little to leeward of our situation in the evening. The night was very dark, with constant hard squalls and heavy rain.

Tuesday, the 19th, no ships in sight. About ten o'clock in the morning it fell calm, with very hard rain and a heavy swell; struck our masts and pulled, not being able to see the land, steered by the swell. When the weather broke up, found we had drifted several miles to leeward. During the calm a fresh breeze springing up, made sail, and endeavored to reach the weather-shore, and anchor with six muskets we had lashed together for that purpose. Finding the boat made no way against the swell and tide, bore up for a bay to leeward, and anchored about 1 a.m. close under the land in five or six fathoms water, blowing fresh, with hard rain.

Wednesday, the 20th, at daylight, supposing the flood-tide making, weighed and stood over to the weather-land, but found we were drifting fast to leeward. About ten o'clock perceived two Chinese boats steering for us. Bore up, and stood towards them, and made signals to induce them to come within hail; on nearing them, they bore up, and passed to leeward of the islands. The Chinese we had in the boat advised me to follow them, and he would take us to Macao by the leeward passage. I expressed my fears of being taken by the Ladrones. Our ammunition being wet, and the muskets rendered useless, we had nothing to defend ourselves with but cutlasses, and in too distressed a situation to make much resistance with them, having been constantly wet, and eaten nothing but a few green oranges for three days.

As our present situation was a hopeless one, and the man assured me there was no fear of encountering any Ladrones, I complied with his request, and stood in to leeward of the islands, where we found the water much smoother, and apparently a direct passage to Macao. We continued pulling and sailing all day. At six o'clock in the evening I discovered three large boats at anchor in a bay to leeward. On seeing us they weighed and made sail towards us. The Chinese said they were Ladrones, and that if they captured us they would most certainly put us all to death! Finding they gained fast on us, struck the masts, and pulled head to wind for five or six hours. The tide turning against us, anchored close under the land to avoid being seen. Soon after we saw the boats pass us to leeward.

Thursday, the 21st, at daylight, the flood tide making, weighed and pulled along shore in great spirits, expecting to be at Macao in two or three hours, as by the Chinese account it was not above six or seven miles distant. After pulling a mile or two perceived several people on shore, standing close to the beach; they were armed with pikes and lances. I ordered the interpreter to hail them, and ask the most direct passage to Macao. They said if we came on shore they would inform us; not liking their hostile appearance, I did not think proper to comply with the request. Saw a large fleet of boats at anchor close under the opposite shore. Our interpreter said they were fishing-boats, and that by going there we should not only get provisions, but a pilot also to take us to Macao.

I bore up, and on nearing them perceived there were some large vessels, very full of men, and mounted with several guns. I hesitated to approach nearer; but the Chinese assuring me they were Mandarine junks and salt-boats, we stood close to one of them, and asked the way to Macao. They gave no answer, but made some signs to us to go in shore. We passed on, and a large rowboat pulled after us; she soon came alongside, when about twenty savage-looking villains, who were stowed at the bottom of the boat, leaped on board us. They were armed with a short sword in each hand, one of which they laid on our necks, and the other pointed to our breasts, keeping their eyes fixed on their officer, waiting his signal to cut or desist. Seeing we were incapable of making any resistance, he sheathed his sword, and the others immediately followed his example.

They then dragged us into their boat, and carried us on board one of their junks, with the most savage demonstrations of joy, and as we supposed, to torture and put us to a cruel death. When on board the junk, they searched all our pockets, took the handkerchiefs from our necks, and brought heavy chains to chain us to the guns.

At this time a boat came, and took me, with one of my men and the interpreter, on board the chief's vessel. I was then taken before the chief. He was seated on deck, in a large chair, dressed in purple silk, with a black turban on. He appeared to be about thirty years of age, a stout commanding-looking man. He took me by the coat, and drew me close to him; then questioned the interpreter very strictly, asking who we were, and what was our business in that part of the country. I told him to say we were Englishmen in distress, having been four days at sea without provisions. This he would not credit, but said we were bad men, and that he would put us all to death; and then ordered some men to put the interpreter to the torture until he confessed the truth.

Upon this occasion, a Ladrone, who had been once to England and spoke a few words of English, came to the chief, and told him we were really Englishmen, and that we had plenty of money, adding that the buttons on my coat were gold. The chief then ordered us some coarse brown rice, of which we made a tolerable meal, having eaten nothing for nearly four days except a few green oranges. During our repast, a number of Ladrones crowded round us, examining our clothes and hair, and giving us every possible annoyance. Several of them brought swords, and laid them on our necks, making signs that they would soon take us on shore, and cut us in pieces, which I am sorry to say was the fate of some hundreds during my captivity.

I was now summoned before the chief, who had been conversing with the interpreter; he said I must write to my captain, and tell him if he did not send a hundred thousand dollars for our ransom, in ten days he would put us all to death. In vain did I assure him it was useless writing unless he would agree to take a much smaller sum; saying we were all poor men, and the most we could possibly raise would not exceed two thousand dollars. Finding that he was much exasperated at my expostulations, I embraced the offer of writing to inform my commander of our unfortunate situation, though there appeared not the least probability of relieving us. They said the letter should be conveyed to Macao in a fishing-boat, which would bring an answer in the morning. A small boat accordingly came alongside, and took the letter.

About six o'clock in the evening they gave us some rice and a little salt fish, which we ate, and they made signs for us to lay down on the deck to sleep; but such numbers of Ladrones were constantly coming from different vessels to see us, and examine our clothes and hair, they would not allow us a moment's quiet. They were particularly anxious for the buttons of my coat, which were new, and as they supposed, gold. I took it off, and laid it on the deck to avoid being disturbed by them; it was taken away in the night, and I saw it on the next day stripped of its buttons.

About nine o'clock a boat came and hailed the chief's vessel; he immediately hoisted his mainsail, and the fleet weighed apparently in great confusion. They worked to windward all night and part of the next day, and anchored about one o'clock in a bay under the island of Lantow, where the head admiral of the Ladrones was lying at anchor, with about two hundred vessels and a Portuguese brig they had captured a few days before, and murdered the captain and part of the crew.

Saturday, the 23d, early in the morning, a fishing-boat came to the fleet to inquire if they had captured a European boat; being answered in the affirmative, they came to the vessel I was in. One of them spoke a few words of English, and told me he had a Ladrone-pass, and was sent by Captain Kay in search of us; I was rather surprised to find he had no letter. He appeared to be well acquainted with the chief, and remained in his cabin smoking opium, and playing cards all the day.

In the evening I was summoned with the interpreter before the chief. He questioned us in a much milder tone, saying he now believed we were Englishmen, a people he wished to be friendly with; and that if our captain would lend him seventy thousand dollars 'till he returned from his cruise up the river, he would repay him, and send us all to Macao. I assured him it was useless writing on those terms, and unless our ransom was speedily settled, the English fleet would sail, and render our enlargement altogether ineffectual. He remained determined, and said if it were not sent, he would keep us, and make us fight, or put us to death. I accordingly wrote, and gave my letter to the man belonging to the boat before mentioned. He said he could not return with an answer in less than five days.

The chief now gave me the letter I wrote when first taken. I have never been able to ascertain his reasons for detaining it, but suppose he dare not negotiate for our ransom without orders from the head admiral, who I understood was sorry at our being captured. He said the English ships would join the Mandarines and attack them. He told the chief that captured us to dispose of us as he pleased.

Monday, the 24th, it blew a strong gale, with constant hard rain; we suffered much from the cold and wet, being obliged to remain on deck with no covering but an old mat, which was frequently taken from us in the night by the Ladrones who were on watch. During the night the Portuguese who were left in the brig murdered the Ladrones that were on board of her, cut the cables, and fortunately escaped through the darkness of the night. I have since been informed they ran her on shore near Macao.

Tuesday, the 25th, at daylight in the morning, the fleet, amounting to about five hundred sail of different sizes, weighed, to proceed on their intended cruise up the rivers, to levy contributions on the towns and villages. It is impossible to describe what were my feelings at this critical time, having received no answers to my letters, and the fleet under-way to sail hundreds of miles up a country never visited by Europeans, there to remain probably for many months, which would render all opportunities of negotiating for our enlargement totally ineffectual; as the only method of communication is by boats that have a pass from the Ladrones, and they dare not venture above twenty miles from Macao, being obliged to come and go in the night, to avoid the Mandarines; and if these boats should be detected in having any intercourse with the Ladrones, they are immediately put to death, and all their relations, though they had not joined in the crime, share in the punishment, in order that not a single person of their families should be left to imitate their crimes or revenge their death. This severity renders communication both dangerous and expensive; no boat would venture out for less than a hundred Spanish dollars.

Wednesday, the 26th, at daylight, we passed in sight of our ships at anchor under the island of Chun Po. The chief then called me, pointed to the ships, and told the interpreter to tell us to look at them, for we should never see them again. About noon we entered a river to the westward of the Bogue, three or four miles from the entrance. We passed a large town situated on the side of a beautiful hill, which is tributary to the Ladrones; the inhabitants saluted them with songs as they passed.

The fleet now divided into two squadrons (the red and the black) and sailed up different branches of the river. At midnight the division we were in anchored close to an immense hill, on the top of which a number of fires were burning, which at daylight I perceived proceeded from a Chinese camp. At the back of the hill was a most beautiful town, surrounded by water, and embellished with groves of orange trees. The chop-house (custom-house) and a few cottages were immediately plundered, and burned down; most of the inhabitants, however, escaped to the camp.

The Ladrones now prepared to attack the town with a formidable force, collected in rowboats from the different vessels. They sent a messenger to the town, demanding a tribute of ten thousand dollars annually, saying if these terms were not complied with they would land, destroy the town, and murder all the inhabitants; which they would certainly have done had the town laid in a more advantageous situation for their purpose; but being placed out of the reach of their shot, they allowed them to come to terms. The inhabitants agreed to pay six thousand dollars, which they were to collect by the time of our return down the river. This finesse had the desired effect, for during our absence they mounted a few guns on a hill, which commanded the passage, and gave us in lieu of the dollars a warm salute on our return.

October the 1st, the fleet weighed in the night, dropped by the tide up the river, and anchored very quietly before a town surrounded by a thick wood. Early in the morning the Ladrones assembled in rowboats and landed; then gave a shout and rushed into the town, sword in hand. The inhabitants fled to the adjacent hills, in numbers apparently superior to the Ladrones. We may easily imagine to ourselves the horror with which these miserable people must be seized, on being obliged to leave their homes and everything dear to them. It was a most melancholy sight to see women in tears, clasping their infants in their arms, and imploring mercy for them from those brutal robbers! The old and the sick, who were unable to fly, or to make resistance, were either made prisoners or most inhumanly butchered! The boats continued passing and repassing from the junks to the shore, in quick succession, laden with booty, and the men besmeared with blood! Two hundred and fifty women, and several children, were made prisoners, and sent on board different vessels. They were unable to escape with the men, owing to that abominable practice of cramping their feet: Several of them were not able to move without assistance, in fact, they might all be said to totter, rather than walk. Twenty of these poor women were sent on board the vessel I was in; they were hauled on board by the hair, and treated in a most savage manner.

When the chief came on board, he questioned them respecting the circumstances of their friends, and demanded ransoms accordingly, from six thousand to six hundred dollars each. He ordered them a berth on deck, at the after part of the vessel, where they had nothing to shelter them from the weather, which at this time was very variable—the days excessively hot, and the nights cold, with heavy rains. The town being plundered of every thing valuable, it was set on fire, and reduced to ashes by the morning. The fleet remained here three days, negotiating for the ransom of the prisoners, and plundering the fish-tanks and gardens. During all this time, the Chinese never ventured from the hills, though there were frequently not more than a hundred Ladrones on shore at a time, and I am sure the people on the hills exceeded ten times that number.

October 5th, the fleet proceeded up another branch of the river, stopping at several small villages to receive tribute, which was generally paid in dollars, sugar, and rice, with a few large pigs roasted whole, as presents for their joss (the idol they worship). Every person, on being ransomed, is obliged to present him with a pig, or some fowls, which the priest offers him with prayers; it remains before him a few hours, and is then divided amongst the crew.

Nothing particular occurred 'till the 10th, except frequent skirmishes on shore between small parties of Ladrones and Chinese soldiers. They frequently obliged my men to go on shore, and fight with the muskets we had when taken, which did great execution, the Chinese principally using bows and arrows. They have match-locks, but use them very unskillfully.

On the 10th, we formed a junction with the black squadron, and proceeded many miles up a wide and beautiful river, passing several ruins of villages that had been destroyed by the black squadron. On the 17th, the fleet anchored abreast four mud batteries, which defended a town so entirely surrounded with wood that it was impossible to form any idea of its size. The weather was very hazy, with hard squalls of rain. The Ladrones remained perfectly quiet for two days. On the third day the forts commenced a brisk fire for several hours: The Ladrones did not return a single shot, but weighed in the night and dropped down the river.

The reasons they gave for not attacking the town, or returning the fire, were that Joss had not promised them success. They are very superstitious, and consult their idol on all occasions.

If his omens are good, they will undertake the most daring enterprizes.

The fleet now anchored opposite the ruins of the town where the women had been made prisoners. Here we remained five or six days, during which time about a hundred of the women were ransomed; the remainder were offered for sale amongst the Ladrones, for forty dollars each. The woman is considered the lawful wife of the purchaser, who would be put to death if he discarded her. Several of them leaped overboard and drowned themselves, rather than submit to such infamous degradation.

The fleet then weighed and made sail down the river, to receive the ransom from the town before mentioned. As we passed the hill, they fired several shots at us, but without effect. The Ladrones were much exasperated, and determined to revenge themselves; they dropped out of reach of their shot, and anchored. Every junk sent about a hundred men each on shore, to cut paddy and destroy their orange-groves, which was most effectually performed for several miles down the river. During our stay here, they received information of nine boats lying up a creek, laden with paddy; boats were immediately dispatched after them.

Next morning these boats were brought to the fleet; ten or twelve men were taken in them. As these had made no resistance, the chief said he would allow them to become Ladrones, if they agreed to take the usual oaths before Joss. Three or four of them refused to comply, for which they were punished in the following cruel manner: their hands were tied behind their back, a rope from the mast-head rove through their arms, and hoisted three or four feet from the deck, and five or six men flogged them with three rattans twisted together 'till they were apparently dead; then hoisted them up to the mast-head, and left them hanging nearly an hour, then lowered them down, and repeated the punishment, 'till they died or complied with the oath.

October the 20th, in the night, an express-boat came with the information that a large Mandarine fleet was proceeding up the river to attack us. The chief immediately weighed, with fifty of the largest vessels, and sailed down the river to meet them. About one in the morning they commenced a heavy fire till daylight, when an express was sent for the remainder of the fleet to join them: about an hour after a counter-order to anchor came, the Mandarine fleet having run. Two or three hours afterwards the chief returned with three captured vessels in tow, having sunk two, and eighty-three sail made their escape. The admiral of the Mandarines blew his vessel up by throwing a lighted match into the magazine as the Ladrones were boarding her; she ran onshore, and they succeeded in getting twenty of her guns.

In this action very few prisoners were taken: the men belonging to the captured vessels drowned themselves, as they were sure of suffering a lingering and cruel death if taken after making resistance. The admiral left the fleet in charge of his brother, the second in command, and proceeded with his own vessel towards Lantow. The fleet remained in this river, cutting paddy, and getting the necessary supplies.

On the 28th of October, I received a letter from Captain Kay, brought by a fisherman, who had told him he would get us all back for three thousand dollars. He advised me to offer three thousand, and if not accepted, extend it to four; but not farther, as it was bad policy to offer much at first: at the same time assuring me we should be liberated, let the ransom be what it would. I offered the chief the three thousand, which he disdainfully refused, saying he was not to be played with; and unless they sent ten thousand dollars, and two large guns, with several casks of gunpowder, he would soon put us all to death. I wrote to Captain Kay, and informed him of the chief's determination, requesting if an opportunity offered to send us a shift of clothes, for which it may be easily imagined we were much distressed, having been seven weeks without a shift; although constantly exposed to the weather and, of course, frequently wet.

On the first of November, the fleet sailed up a narrow river, and anchored at night within two miles of a town called Little Whampoa. In front of it was a small fort, and several Mandarine vessels lying in the harbor. The chief sent the interpreter to me, saying I must order my men to make cartridges and clean their muskets, ready to go on shore in the morning. I assured the interpreter I should give the men no such orders, that they must please themselves. Soon after the chief came on board, threatening to put us all to a cruel death if we refused to obey his orders. For my own part I remained determined, and advised the men not to comply, as I thought by making ourselves useful we should be accounted too valuable.

A few hours afterwards he sent to me again, saying that if myself and the quartermaster would assist them at the great guns, that if also the rest of the men went on shore and succeeded in taking the place, he would then take the money offered for our ransom, and give them twenty dollars for every Chinaman's head they cut off. To these proposals we cheerfully acceded, in hopes of facilitating our deliverance.

Early in the morning the forces intended for landing were assembled in rowboats, amounting in the whole to three or four thousand men. The largest vessels weighed and hauled in shore, to cover the landing of the forces and attack the fort and Mandarine vessels. About nine o'clock the action commenced, and continued with great spirit for nearly an hour, when the walls of the fort gave way, and the men retreated in the greatest confusion.

The Mandarine vessels still continued firing, having blocked up the entrance of the harbor to prevent the Ladrone boats entering. At this the Ladrones were much exasperated, and about three hundred of them swam on shore, with a short sword lashed close under each arm; they then ran along the banks of the river 'till they came abreast of the vessels, and then swam off again and boarded them. The Chinese, thus attacked, leaped overboard and endeavored to reach the opposite shore; the Ladrones followed, and cut the greater number of them to pieces in the water. They next towed the vessels out of the harbor, and attacked the town with increased fury. The inhabitants fought about a quarter of an hour, and then retreated to an adjacent hill, from which they were soon driven with great slaughter.

After this the Ladrones returned, and plundered the town, every boat leaving it when laden. The Chinese on the hills, perceiving most of the boats were off, rallied and retook the town, after killing near two hundred Ladrones. One of my men was unfortunately lost in this dreadful massacre! The Ladrones landed a second time, drove the Chinese out of the town, then reduced it to ashes, and put all their prisoners to death, without regarding either age or sex!

I must not omit to mention a most horrid (though ludicrous) circumstance which happened at this place. The Ladrones were paid by their chief ten dollars for every Chinaman's head they produced. One of my men turning the corner of a street was met by a Ladrone running furiously after a Chinese; he had a drawn sword in his hand, and two Chinaman's heads which he had cut off, tied by their tails, and slung round his neck. I was witness myself to some of them producing five or six to obtain payment!

On the 4th of November an order arrived from the admiral for the fleet to proceed immediately to Lantow, where he was lying with only two vessels, and three Portuguese ships and a brig constantly annoying him; several sail of Mandarine vessels were daily expected. The fleet weighed and proceeded towards Lantow. On passing the island of Lintin, three ships and a brig gave chase to us. The Ladrones prepared to board; but night closing we lost sight of them: I am convinced they altered their course and stood from us. These vessels were in the pay of the Chinese government, and style themselves the Invincible Squadron, cruising in the river Tigris to annihilate the Ladrones!

On the fifth, in the morning, the red squadron anchored in a bay under Lantow; the black squadron stood to the eastward. In this bay they hauled several of their vessels on shore to bream their bottoms and repair them.

In the afternoon of the 8th of November, four ships, a brig and a schooner came off the mouth of the bay. At first the pirates were much alarmed, supposing them to be English vessels come to rescue us. Some of them threatened to hang us to the masthead for them to fire at; and with much difficulty we persuaded them that they were Portuguese. The Ladrones had only seven junks in a fit state for action; these they hauled outside, and moored them head and stern across the bay; and manned all the boats belonging to the repairing vessels ready for boarding.

The Portuguese, observing these maneuvers, hove to, and communicated by boats. Soon afterwards they made sail, each ship firing her broadside as she passed, but without effect, the shot falling far short. The Ladrones did not return a single shot, but waved their colors, and threw up rockets, to induce them to come further in, which they might easily have done, the outside junks lying in four fathoms water which I sounded myself: though the Portuguese in their letters to Macao lamented there was not sufficient water for them to engage closer, but that they would certainly prevent their escaping before the Mandarine fleet arrived!

On the 20th of November, early in the morning, I perceived an immense fleet of Mandarine vessels standing for the bay. On nearing us, they formed a line and stood close in; each vessel as she discharged her guns tacked to join the rear and reload. They kept up a constant fire for about two hours, when one of their largest vessels was blown up by a firebrand thrown from a Ladrone junk; after which they kept at a more respectful distance, but continued firing without intermission 'till the 21st at night, when it fell calm.

The Ladrones towed out seven large vessels, with about two hundred rowboats to board them; but a breeze springing up, they made sail and escaped. The Ladrones returned into the bay, and anchored. The Portuguese and Mandarines followed, and continued a heavy cannonading during that night and the next day. The vessel I was in had her foremast shot away, which they supplied very expeditiously by taking a mainmast from a smaller vessel.

On the 23d, in the evening, it again fell calm; the Ladrones towed out fifteen junks in two divisions, with the intention of surrounding them, which was nearly effected, having come up with and boarded one, when a breeze suddenly sprung up. The captured vessel mounted twenty-two guns. Most of her crew leaped overboard; sixty or seventy were taken immediately, cut to pieces and thrown into the river. Early in the morning the Ladrones returned into the bay, and anchored in the same situation as before. The Portuguese and Mandarines followed, keeping up a constant fire. The Ladrones never returned a single shot, but always kept in readiness to board, and the Portuguese were careful never to allow them an opportunity.

On the 28th, at night, they sent in eight fire-vessels, which if properly constructed must have done great execution, having every advantage they could wish for to effect their purpose; a strong breeze and tide directly into the bay, and the vessels lying so close together that it was impossible to miss them. On their first appearance the Ladrones gave a general shout, supposing them to be Mandarine vessels on fire, but were very soon convinced of their mistake. They came very regularly into the center of the fleet, two and two, burning furiously; one of them came alongside of the vessel I was in, but they succeeded in booming her off. She appeared to be a vessel of about thirty tons; her hold was filled with straw and wood, and there were a few small boxes of combustibles on her deck, which exploded alongside of us without doing any damage. The Ladrones, however, towed them all on shore, extinguished the fires, and broke them up for fire-wood. The Portuguese claim the credit of constructing these destructive machines, and actually sent a dispatch to the Governor of Macao, saying they had destroyed at least one-third of the Ladrones' fleet, and hoped soon to effect their purpose by totally annihilating them!

On the 29th of November, the Ladrones being all ready for sea, they weighed and stood boldly out, bidding defiance to the invincible squadron and imperial fleet, consisting of ninety-three war-junks, six Portuguese ships, a brig, and a schooner. Immediately the Ladrones weighed, they made all sail. The Mandarines and Portuguese chased them two or three hours, keeping up a constant fire; finding they did not come up with them, they hauled their wind and stood to the eastward.

Thus terminated the boasted blockade, which lasted nine days, during which time the Ladrones completed all their repairs. In this action not a single Ladrone vessel was destroyed, and their loss about thirty or forty men. An American was also killed, one of three that remained out of eight taken in a schooner. I had two very narrow escapes: the first, a twelve-pounder shot fell within three or four feet of me; another took a piece out of a small brass-swivel on which I was standing. The chief's wife frequently sprinkled me with garlic-water, which they consider an effectual charm against shot. The fleet continued under sail all night, steering towards the eastward. In the morning they anchored in a large bay surrounded by lofty and barren mountains.

On the 2nd of December I received a letter from Lieutenant Maughn, commander of the Honorable Company's cruiser *Antelope,* saying that he had the ransom on board, and had been three days cruising after us, and wished me to settle with the chief on the securest method of delivering it. The chief agreed to send us in a small gunboat, 'till we came within sight of the *Antelope;* then the Compradore's boat was to bring the ransom and receive us.

I was so agitated at receiving this joyful news that it was with considerable difficulty I could scrawl about two or three lines to inform Lieutenant Maughn of the arrangements I had made. We were all so deeply affected by the gratifying tidings that we seldom closed our eyes, but continued watching day and night for the boat. On the 6th she returned with Lieutenant Maughn's answer, saying he would respect any single boat; but would not allow the fleet to approach him. The chief then, according to his first proposal, ordered a gunboat to take us, and with no small degree of pleasure we left the Ladrone fleet about four o'clock in the morning.

At one p.m. saw the *Antelope* under all sail, standing toward us. The Ladrone boat immediately anchored, and dispatched the Compradore's boat for the ransom, saying that if she approached nearer, they would return to the fleet; and they were just weighing when she shortened sail, and anchored about two miles from us. The boat did not reach her 'till late in the afternoon, owing to the tide's being strong against her. She received the ransom and left the *Antelope* just before dark. A Mandarine boat that had been lying concealed under the land and watching their maneuvers gave chase to her, and was within a few fathoms of taking her when she saw a light, which the Ladrones answered, and the Mandarine hauled off.

Our situation was now a most critical one; the ransom was in the hands of the Ladrones, and the Compradore dare not return with us for fear of a second attack from the Mandarine boat. The Ladrones would not remain 'till morning, so we were obliged to return with them to the fleet.

In the morning the chief inspected the ransom, which consisted of the following articles: two bales of superfine scarlet cloth; two chests of opium; two casks of gunpowder; and a telescope; the rest in dollars. He objected to the telescope not being new; and said he should detain one of us 'till another was sent, or a hundred dollars in lieu of it. The Compradore, however, agreed with him for the hundred dollars.

Every thing being at length settled, the chief ordered two gunboats to convey us near the *Antelope;* we saw her just before dusk, when the Ladrone boats left us. We had the inexpressible pleasure of arriving on board the *Antelope* at 7 p.m., where we were most cordially received and heartily congratulated on our safe and happy deliverance from a miserable captivity, which we had endured for eleven weeks and three days.

## A Few Remarks on the Origin, Progress, Manners, and Customs of the Ladrones

The Ladrones are a disaffected race of Chinese that revolted against the oppressions of the Mandarines. They first commenced their depredations on the Western coast (Cochin-China), by attacking small trading vessels in rowboats, carrying from thirty to forty men each. They continued this system of piracy several years; at length their successes, and the oppressive state of the Chinese, had the effect of rapidly increasing their numbers. Hundreds of fishermen and others flocked to their standard; and as their number increased they consequently became more desperate. They blockaded all the principal rivers, and captured several large junks, mounting from ten to fifteen guns each.

With these junks they formed a very formidable fleet, and no small vessels could trade on the coast with safety. They plundered several small villages, and exercised such wanton barbarity as struck horror into the breasts of the Chinese. To check these enormities the government equipped a fleet of forty imperial war-junks, mounting from eighteen to twenty guns each. On the very first rencontre, twenty-eight of the imperial junks struck to the pirates; the rest saved themselves by a precipitate retreat.

These junks, fully equipped for war, were a great acquisition to them. Their numbers augmented so rapidly that at the period of my captivity they were supposed to amount to near seventy thousand men, eight hundred large vessels, and nearly a thousand small ones, including rowboats. They were divided into five squadrons, distinguished by different colored flags: Each squadron commanded by an admiral, or chief; but all under the orders of A-juo-Chay, their premier chief, a most daring and enterprising man, who went so far as to declare his intention of displacing the present Tartar family from the throne of China, and to restore the ancient Chinese dynasty.

This extraordinary character would have certainly shaken the foundation of the government, had he not been thwarted by the jealousy of the second-in-command, who declared his independence, and soon after surrendered to the Mandarines with five hundred vessels on promise of a pardon. Most of the inferior chiefs followed his example. A-juo-Chay held out a few months longer, and at length surrendered with sixteen thousand men, on condition of a general pardon, and himself to be made a Mandarine of distinction.

The Ladrones have no settled residence on shore, but live constantly in their vessels. The after-part is appropriated to the captain and his wives; he generally has five or six. With respect to conjugal rights they are religiously strict; no person is allowed to have a woman on board unless married to her according to their laws. Every man is allowed a small berth, about four feet square, where he stows with his wife and family.

From the number of souls crowded in so small a space, it must naturally be supposed they are horridly dirty, which is evidently the case, and their vessels swarm with all kinds of vermin. Rats in particular, which they encourage to breed, and eat them as great delicacies; in fact, there are very few creatures they will not eat. During our captivity we lived three weeks on caterpillars boiled with rice. They are much addicted to gambling, and spend all their leisure hours at cards and smoking opium.

# The Malay Proas

## *James Fenimore Cooper*

We had cleared the Straits of Sunda early in the morning, and
had made a pretty fair run in the course of the day, though most
of the time in thick weather. Just as the sun set, however, the
horizon became clear, and we got a sight of two small sails,
seemingly heading in toward the coast of Sumatra, proas by their
rig and dimensions. They were so distant, and were so evidently
steering for the land, that no one gave them much thought, or
bestowed on them any particular attention. Proas in that quarter
were usually distrusted by ships, it is true; but the sea is full of
them, and far more are innocent than are guilty of any acts of
violence. Then it became dark soon after these craft were seen,
and night shut them in. An hour after the sun had set, the wind
fell to a light air that just kept steerage-way on the ship. Fortunately, the *John* was not only fast but she minded her helm, as a
light-footed girl turns in a lively dance. I never was in a better-
steering ship, most especially in moderate weather.

Mr. Marble had the middle watch that night, and, of course,
I was on deck from midnight until four in the morning. It proved
misty most of the watch, and for quite an hour we had a light

drizzling rain. The ship the whole time was close-hauled, carrying royals. As everybody seemed to have made up his mind to a quiet night, one without any reefing or furling, most of the watch were sleeping about the decks, or wherever they could get good quarters and be least in the way. I do not know what kept me awake, for lads of my age are apt to get all the sleep they can; but I believe I was thinking of Clawbonny, and Grace, and Lucy; for the latter, excellent girl as she was, often crossed my mind in those days of youth and comparative innocence. Awake I was, and walking in the weather-gangway, in a sailor's trot. Mr. Marble, he I do believe was fairly snoozing on the hen-coops, being, like the sails, as one might say, barely "asleep." At that moment I heard a noise, one familiar to seamen; that of an oar falling in a boat. So completely was my mind bent on other and distant scenes, that at first I felt no surprise, as if we were in a harbor surrounded by craft of various sizes, coming and going at all hours. But a second thought destroyed this illusion, and I looked eagerly about me. Directly on our weather-bow, distant, perhaps, a cable's length, I saw a small sail, and I could distinguish it sufficiently well to perceive it was a proa. I sang out "Sail ho! And close aboard!"

Mr. Marble was on his feet in an instant. He afterward told me that when he opened his eyes, for he admitted this much to me in confidence, they fell directly on the stranger. He was too much of a seaman to require a second look in order to ascertain what was to be done. "Keep the ship away—keep her broad off!" he called out to the man at the wheel. "Lay the yards square— call all hands, one of you. Captain Robbins, Mr. Kite, bear a hand up; the bloody proas are aboard us!" The last part of this call was uttered in a loud voice, with the speaker's head down the companion-way. It was heard plainly enough below, but scarcely at all on deck.

In the meantime everybody was in motion. It is amazing how soon sailors are wide awake when there is really anything to do! It appeared to me that all our people mustered on deck in less than a minute, most of them with nothing on but their shirts and trousers. The ship was nearly before the wind by the time I heard the captain's voice; and then Mr. Kite came bustling in among us forward, ordering most of the men to lay aft to the braces, remaining himself on the forecastle, and keeping me with him to let go the sheets. On the forecastle, the strange sail was no longer visible, being now abaft the beam; but I could hear Mr. Marble swearing there were two of them, and that they must be the very chaps we had seen to leeward, and standing in for the land at sunset. I also heard the captain calling out to the steward to bring him a powder-horn.

Immediately after, orders were given to let fly all our sheets forward, and then I perceived that they were wearing ship. Nothing saved us but the prompt order of Mr. Marble to keep the ship away, by which means instead of moving toward the proas, we instantly began to move from them. Although they went three feet to our two, this gave us a moment of breathing time.

As our sheets were all flying forward, and remained so for a few minutes, it gave me leisure to look about. I soon saw both proas, and glad enough was I to perceive that they had not approached materially nearer. Mr. Kite observed this also, and remarked that our movements had been so prompt as to "take the rascals aback." He meant they did not exactly know what we were at, and had not kept away with us.

At this instant, the captain and five or six of the oldest seamen began to cast loose all our starboard, or weather guns, four in all, and sixes. We had loaded these guns in the Straits of Banca with grape and canister, in readiness for just such pirates as were now coming down upon us; and nothing was wanting but the priming and a hot loggerhead. It seems two of the last had been ordered in the fire, when we saw the proas at sunset; and they were now in excellent condition for service, live coals being kept around them all night by command. I saw a cluster of men busy with the second gun from forward, and could distinguish the captain pointing to it.

"There cannot well be any mistake, Mr. Marble?" the captain observed, hesitating whether to fire or not.

"Mistake, sir? Lord, Captain Robbins, you might cannonade any of the islands astern for a week, and never hurt an honest man. Let 'em have it, sir; I'll answer for it, you do good."

This settled the matter. The loggerhead was applied, and one of our sixes spoke out in a smart report. A breathless stillness succeeded. The proas did not alter their course, but neared us fast. The captain levelled his night-glass, and I heard him tell Kite, in a low voice, that they were full of men. The word was now passed to clear away all the guns, and to open the arm-chest, to come at the muskets and pistols. I heard the rattling of the boarding-pikes, too, as they were cut adrift from the spanker-boom and fell upon the decks. All this sounded very ominous, and I began to think we should have a desperate engagement first, and then have all our throats cut afterward.

I expected now to hear the guns discharged in quick succession, but they were got ready only, not fired. Kite went aft, and returned with three or four muskets, and as many pikes. He gave the latter to those of the people who had nothing to do with the guns. By this time the ship was on a wind, steering a good full, while the two proas were just abeam, and closing fast. The stillness that reigned on both sides was like that of death. The proas, however, fell a little more astern; the result of their own maneuvering, out of all doubt, as they moved through the water much faster than the ship, seeming desirous of dropping into our wake, with a design of closing under our stern and avoiding our broadside. As this would never do, and the wind freshened so as to give us four or five knot way, a most fortunate circumstance for us, the captain determined to tack while he had room.

The *John* behaved beautifully, and came round like a top. The proas saw there was no time to lose, and attempted to close before we could fill again; and this they would have done with ninety-nine ships in a hundred. The captain knew his vessel, however, and did not let her lose her way, making everything draw again as it might be by instinct. The proas tacked too and, laying up much nearer to the wind than we did, appeared as if about to close on our lee-bow. The question was, now, whether we could pass them or not before they got near enough to grapple. If the pirates got on board us, we were hopelessly gone; and everything depended on coolness and judgment. The captain behaved perfectly well in this critical instant, commanding a dead silence, and the closest attention to his orders.

I was too much interested at this moment to feel the concern that I might otherwise have experienced. On the forecastle, it appeared to us all that we should be boarded in a minute, for one of the proas was actually within a hundred feet, though losing her advantage a little by getting under the lee of our sails. Kite had ordered us to muster forward of the rigging, to meet the expected leap with a discharge of muskets and then to present our pikes, when I felt an arm thrown around my body and was turned inboard, while another person assumed my place.

This was Neb, who had thus coolly thrust himself before me, in order to meet the danger first. I felt vexed, even while touched with the fellow's attachment and self-devotion, but had no time to betray either feeling before the crews of the proas gave a yell, and discharged some fifty or sixty matchlocks at us. The air was full of bullets, but they all went over our heads. Not a soul on board the *John* was hurt. On our side, we gave the gentlemen the four sixes, two at the nearest and two at the stern-most proa, which was still near a cable's length distant. As often happens, the one seemingly farthest from danger fared the worst. Our grape and canister had room to scatter, and I can at this distant day still hear the shrieks that arose from that craft! They were like the yells of fiends in anguish. The effect on that proa was instantaneous; instead of keeping on after her consort, she wore short round on her heel, and stood away in our wake, on the other tack, apparently to get out of the range of our fire.

I doubt if we touched a man in the nearest proa. At any rate, no noise proceeded from her, and she came up under our bows fast. As every gun was discharged, and there was not time to load them, all now depended on repelling the boarders. Part of our people mustered in the waist, where it was expected the proa would fall alongside, and part on the forecastle. Just as this distribution was made, the pirates cast their grapnel. It was admirably thrown, but caught only by a ratlin. I saw this, and was about to jump into the rigging to try what I could do to clear it, when Neb again went ahead of me, and cut the ratlin with his knife. This was just as the pirates had abandoned sails and oars, and had risen to haul up alongside. So sudden was the release that twenty of them fell over by their own efforts. In this state the ship passed ahead, all her canvas being full, leaving the proa motionless in her wake. In passing, however, the two vessels were so near that those aft in the *John* distinctly saw the swarthy faces of their enemies.

We were no sooner clear of the proas than the order was given, "Ready about!" The helm was put down, and the ship came into the wind in a minute. As we came square with the two proas, all our larboard guns were given to them, and this ended the affair. I think the nearest of the rascals got it this time, for away she went, after her consort, both running off toward the islands. We made a little show of chasing, but it was only a feint; for we were too glad to get away from them, to be in earnest. In ten minutes after we tacked the last time, we ceased firing, having thrown some eight or ten round-shot after the proas, and were close-hauled again, heading to the southwest.

We were clear.

# The Granddaughter of the Great Mogul

## *Daniel Defoe*

In this time I pursued my voyage, coasted the whole Malabar shore, and met with no purchase but a great Portugal East India ship, which I chased into Goa, where she got out of my reach. I took several small vessels and barks, but little of value in them, till I entered the great Bay of Bengal, when I began to look about me with more expectation of success, though without prospect of what happened.

I cruised here about two months, finding nothing worth while; so I stood away to a port on the north point of the isle of Sumatra, where I made no stay; for here I got news that two large ships belonging to the Great Mogul were expected to cross the bay from Hoogly, in the Ganges, to the country of the King of Pegu, being to carry the granddaughter of the Great Mogul to Pegu, who was to be married to the king of that country, with all her retinue, jewels, and wealth.

This was a booty worth watching for, though it had been some months longer; so I resolved that we would go and cruise off Point Negaris, on the east side of the bay, near Diamond Isle; and here we plied off and on for three weeks, and began to despair of success; but the knowledge of the booty we expected spurred us on, and we waited with great patience, for we knew the prize would be immensely rich.

At length we spied three ships coming right up to us with the wind. We could easily see they were not Europeans by their sails, and began to prepare ourselves for a prize, not for a fight; but were a little disappointed when we found the first ship full of guns and full of soldiers, and in condition, had she been managed by English sailors, to have fought two such ships as ours were. However, we resolved to attack her if she had been full of devils as she was full of men.

Accordingly, when we came near them, we fired a gun with shot as a challenge. They fired again immediately three or four guns, but fired them so confusedly that we could easily see they did not understand their business; when we considered how to lay them on board, and so to come thwart them, if we could; but falling, for want of wind, open to them, we gave them a fair broadside. We could easily see, by the confusion that was on board, that they were frightened out of their wits; they fired here a gun and there a gun, and some on that side that was from us, as well as those that were next to us. The next thing we did was to lay them on board, which we did presently, and then gave them a volley of our small shot, which, as they stood so thick, killed a great many of them, and made all the rest run down under their hatches, crying out like creatures bewitched. In a word, we presently took the ship, and having secured her men, we chased the other two. One was chiefly filled with women, and the other with lumber. Upon the whole, as the granddaughter of the Great

Mogul was our prize in the first ship, so in the second was her women, or, in a word, her household, her eunuchs, all the necessaries of her wardrobe, of her stables, and of her kitchen; and in the last, great quantities of household stuff, and things less costly, though not less useful.

But the first was the main prize. When my men had entered and mastered the ship, one of our lieutenants called for me, and accordingly I jumped on board. He told me he thought nobody but I ought to go into the great cabin, or, at least, nobody should go there before me; for that the lady herself and all her attendance was there, and he feared the men were so heated they would murder them all, or do worse.

I immediately went to the great cabin door, taking the lieutenant that called me along with me, and caused the cabin door to be opened. But such a sight of glory and misery was never seen by a buccaneer before. The queen (for such she was to have been) was all in gold and silver, but frightened and crying, and, at the sight of me, she appeared trembling, and just as if she was going to die. She sat on the side of a kind of a bed like a couch, with no canopy over it, or any covering; only made to lie down upon. She was, in a manner, covered with diamonds, and I, like a true pirate, soon let her see that I had more mind to the jewels than to the lady.

However, before I touched her, I ordered the lieutenant to place a guard at the cabin door, and fastening the door, shut us both in, which he did. The lady was young, and, I suppose, in their country esteem, very handsome, but she was not very much so in my thoughts. At first her fright, and the danger she thought she was in of being killed, taught her to do everything that she thought might interpose between her and danger, and that was to take off her jewels as fast as she could, and give them to me; and I, without any great compliment, took them as fast as she gave them me, and put them into my pocket, taking no great notice of them or of her, which frighted her worse than all the rest, and she said something which I could not understand. However, two of the other ladies came, all crying, and kneeled down to me with their hands lifted up. What they meant, I knew not at first; but by their gestures and pointings I found at last it was to beg the young queen's life, and that I would not kill her.

When the three ladies kneeled down to me, and as soon as I understood what it was for, I let them know I would not hurt the queen, nor let any one else hurt her, but that she must give me all her jewels and money. Upon this they acquainted her that I would save her life; and no sooner had they assured her of that but she got up smiling, and went to a fine Indian cabinet, and opened a private drawer, from whence she took another little thing full of little square drawers and holes. This she brings to me in her hand, and offered to kneel down to give it me. This innocent usage began to rouse some good-nature in me (though I never had much), and I would not let her kneel; but sitting down myself on the side of her couch or bed, made a motion to her to sit down too. But here she was frightened again, it seems, at what I had no thought of. But as I did not offer anything of that kind, only made her sit down by me, they began all to be easier after some time, and she gave me the little box or casket, I know not what to call it, but it was full of invaluable jewels. I

and eat, which she did, but with so much ceremony that I did not know well what to do with it.

After we had eaten, she rose up again and, drinking some water out of a china cup, sat her down on the side of the couch as before. When she saw I had done eating, she went then to another cabinet, and pulling out a drawer, she brought it to me; it was full of small pieces of gold coin of Pegu, about as big as an English half-guinea, and I think there were three thousand of them. She opened several other drawers, and showed me the wealth that was in them, and then gave me the key of the whole.

We had revelled thus all day, and part of the next day, in a bottomless sea of riches, when my lieutenant began to tell me we must consider what to do with our prisoners and the ships, for that there was no subsisting in that manner. Upon this we called a short council, and concluded to carry the great ship away with us, but to put all the prisoners—queen, ladies, and all the rest—into the lesser vessels and let them go; and so far was I from ravishing this lady, as I hear is reported of me, that though I might rifle her of everything else, yet, I assure you, I let her go untouched for me, or, as I am satisfied, for any one of my men; nay, when we dismissed them, we gave her leave to take a great many things of value with her, which she would have been plundered of if I had not been so careful of her.

We had now wealth enough not only to make us rich, but almost to have made a nation rich; and to tell you the truth, considering the costly things we took here, which we did not know the value of, and besides gold and silver and jewels—I say, we never knew how rich we were; besides which we had a great quantity of bales of goods, as well calicoes as wrought silks, which, being for sale, were perhaps as a cargo of goods to answer the bills which might be drawn upon them for the account of the bride's portion; all which fell into our hands, with a great sum in silver coin, too big to talk of among Englishmen, especially while I am living.

# The Man with the Belt of Gold

## Robert Louis Stevenson

More than a week went by, in which the ill-luck that had hitherto pursued the *Covenant* upon this voyage grew yet more strongly marked. Some days she made a little way; others, she was driven actually back. At last we were beaten so far to the south that we tossed and tacked to and fro the whole of the ninth day, within sight of Cape Wrath and the wild, rocky coast on either hand of it. There followed on that a council of the officers, and some decision which I did not rightly understand, seeing only the result: that we had made a fair wind of a foul one and were running south.

The tenth afternoon there was a falling swell and a thick, wet, white fog that hid one end of the brig from the other. All afternoon, when I went on deck, I saw men and officers listening hard over the bulwarks—"for breakers," they said; and though I did not so much as understand the word, I felt danger in the air, and was excited.

Maybe about ten at night, I was serving Mr. Riach and the captain at their supper, when the ship struck something with a great sound, and we heard voices singing out. My two masters leaped to their feet.

"She's struck!" said Mr. Riach.

"No, sir," said the captain. "We've only run a boat down."

And they hurried out.

The captain was in the right of it. We had run down a boat in the fog, and she had parted in the midst and gone to the bottom with all her crew but one. This man (as I heard afterwards) had been sitting in the stern as a passenger, while the rest were on the benches rowing. At the moment of the blow the stern had been thrown into the air, and the man (having his hands free, and for all he was encumbered with a frieze overcoat that came below his knees) had leaped up and caught hold of the brig's bowsprit. It showed he had luck and much agility and unusual strength, that he should have thus saved himself from such a pass. And yet, when the captain brought him into the round-house, and I set eyes on him for the first time, he looked as cool as I did.

He was smallish in stature, but well set and as nimble as a goat; his face was of a good open expression, but sunburnt very dark, and heavily freckled and pitted with the small-pox; his eyes were unusually light and had a kind of dancing madness in them that was both engaging and alarming; and when he took off his great-coat, he laid a pair of fine silver-mounted pistols on the table, and I saw that he was belted with a great sword. His manners, besides, were elegant, and he pledged the captain handsomely. Altogether I thought of him, at the first sight, that here was a man I would rather call my friend than my enemy.

The captain, too, was taking his observations, but rather of the man's clothes than his person. And to be sure, as soon as he had taken off the great-coat, he showed forth mighty fine for the round-house of a merchant brig, having a hat with feathers, a red waistcoat, breeches of black plush, and a blue coat with silver buttons and handsome silver lace; costly clothes, though somewhat spoiled with the fog and being slept in.

"I'm vexed, sir, about the boat," says the captain.

"There are some pretty men gone to the bottom," said the stranger, "that I would rather see on the dry land again than half a score of boats."

"Friends of yours?" said Hoseason.

"You have none such friends in your country," was the reply. "They would have died for me like dogs."

"Well, sir," said the captain, still watching him, "there are more men in the world than boats to put them in."

"And that's true, too," cried the other, "and ye seem to be a gentleman of great penetration."

"I have been in France, sir," says the captain, so that it was plain he meant more by the words than showed upon the face of them.

"Well, sir," says the other, "and so has many a pretty man, for the matter of that."

"No doubt, sir," says the captain, "and fine coats."

"Oho!" says the stranger, "is that how the wind sets?" And he laid his hand quickly on his pistols.

"Don't be hasty," said the captain. "Don't do a mischief before ye see the need of it. Ye've a French soldier's coat upon your back and a Scotch tongue in your head, to be sure; but so has many an honest fellow in these days, and I dare say none the worse of it."

"So?" said the gentleman in the fine coat: "Are ye of the honest party?" (meaning, Was he a Jacobite? for each side, in these sort of civil broils, takes the name of honesty for its own).

"Why, sir," replied the captain, "I am a true-blue Protestant, and I thank God for it." (It was the first word of any religion I had ever heard from him, but I learnt afterwards he was a great church-goer while on shore.) "But, for all that," says he, "I can be sorry to see another man with his back to the wall."

"Can ye so, indeed?" asked the Jacobite. "Well, sir, to be quite plain with ye, I am one of those honest gentlemen that were in trouble about the years forty-five and six; and (to be still quite plain with ye) if I got into the hands of any of the red-coated gentry, it's like it would go hard with me. Now, sir, I was for France; and there was a French ship cruising here to pick me up; but she gave us the go-by in the fog—as I wish from the heart that ye had done yoursel'! And the best that I can say is this: If ye can set me ashore where I was going, I have that upon me will reward you highly for your trouble."

"In France?" says the captain. "No, sir; that I cannot do. But where ye come from—we might talk of that."

And then, unhappily, he observed me standing in my corner, and packed me off to the galley to get supper for the gentleman. I lost no time, I promise you; and when I came back into the round-house, I found the gentleman had taken a money-belt from about his waist, and poured out a guinea or two upon the table. The captain was looking at the guineas, and then at the belt, and then at the gentleman's face; and I thought he seemed excited.

"Half of it," he cried, "and I'm your man!"

The other swept back the guineas into the belt, and put it on again under his waistcoat. "I have told ye sir," said he, "that not one doit of it belongs to me. It belongs to my chieftain," and here he touched his hat, "and while I would be but a silly messenger to grudge some of it that the rest might come safe, I should show myself a hound indeed if I bought my own carcase any too dear. Thirty guineas on the sea-side, or sixty if ye set me on the Linnhe Loch. Take it, if ye will; if not, ye can do your worst."

"Ay," said Hoseason. "And if I give ye over to the soldiers?"

"Ye would make a fool's bargain," said the other. "My chief, let me tell you, sir, is forfeited, like every honest man in Scotland. His estate is in the hands of the man they call King George; and it is his officers that collect the rents, or try to collect them. But for the honour of Scotland, the poor tenant bodies take a thought upon their chief lying in exile; and this money is a part of that very rent for which King George is looking. Now, sir, ye seem to me to be a man that understands things: Bring this money within the reach of Government, and how much of it'll come to you?"

"Little enough, to be sure," said Hoseason; and then, "If they knew," he added, drily. "But I think, if I was to try, that I could hold my tongue about it."

"Ah, but I'll befool ye there!" cried the gentleman. "Play me false, and I'll play you cunning. If a hand is laid upon me, they shall ken what money it is."

"Well," returned the captain, "what must be must. Sixty guineas, and done. Here's my hand upon it."

"And here's mine," said the other.

And thereupon the captain went out (rather hurriedly, I thought), and left me alone in the round-house with the stranger.

At that period (so soon after the forty-five) there were many exiled gentlemen coming back at the peril of their lives, either to see their friends or to collect a little money; and as for the Highland chiefs that had been forfeited, it was a common matter of talk how their tenants would stint themselves to send them money, and their clansmen outface the soldiery to get it in, and run the gauntlet of our great navy to carry it across. All this I had, of course, heard tell of; and now I had a man under my eyes whose life was forfeit on all these counts and upon one more, for he was not only a rebel and a smuggler of rents, but had taken service with King Louis of France. And as if all this were not enough, he had a belt full of golden guineas round his loins. Whatever my opinions, I could not look on such a man without a lively interest.

"And so you're a Jacobite?" said I, as I set meat before him.

"Ay," said he, beginning to eat. "And you, by your long face, should be a Whig?"

"Betwixt and between," said I, not to annoy him; for indeed I was as good a Whig as Mr. Campbell could make me.

"And that's naething," said he. "But I'm saying, Mr. Betwixt-and-Between," he added, "this bottle of yours is dry; and it's hard if I'm to pay sixty guineas and be grudged a dram upon the back of it."

"I'll go and ask for the key," said I, and stepped on deck.

The fog was as close as ever, but the swell almost down. They had laid the brig to, not knowing precisely where they were, and the wind (what little there was of it) not serving well for their true course. Some of the hands were still hearkening for breakers; but the captain and the two officers were in the waist with their heads together. It struck me (I don't know why) that they were after no good; and the first word I heard, as I drew softly near, more than confirmed me.

It was Mr. Riach, crying out as if upon a sudden thought: "Couldn't we wile him out of the round-house?"

"He's better where he is," returned Hoseason; "He hasn't room to use his sword."

"Well, that's true," said Riach; "but he's hard to come at."

"Hut!" said Hoseason. "We can get the man in talk, one upon each side, and pin him by the two arms; or if that'll not hold, sir, we can make a run by both the doors and get him under hand before he has the time to draw."

At this hearing, I was seized with both fear and anger at these treacherous, greedy, bloody men that I sailed with. My first mind was to run away; my second was bolder.

"Captain," said I, "the gentleman is seeking a dram, and the bottle's out. Will you give me the key?"

They all started and turned about.

"Why, here's our chance to get the firearms!" Riach cried; and then to me: "Hark ye, David," he said, "Do ye ken where the pistols are?"

"Ay, ay," put in Hoseason. "David kens; David's a good lad. Ye see, David my man, yon wild Hielandman is a danger to the ship, besides being a rank foe to King George, God bless him!"

I had never been so be-Davided since I came on board: but I said Yes, as if all I heard were quite natural.

"The trouble is," resumed the captain, "that all our firelocks, great and little, are in the round-house under this man's nose; likewise the powder. Now, if I, or one of the officers, was to go in and take them, he would fall to thinking. But a lad like you, David, might snap up a horn and a pistol or two without remark. And if ye can do it cleverly, I'll bear it in mind when it'll be good for you to have friends; and that's when we come to Carolina."

Here Mr. Riach whispered him a little.

"Very right, sir," said the captain; and then to myself: "And see here, David, yon man has a beltful of gold, and I give you my word that you shall have your fingers in it."

I told him I would do as he wished, though indeed I had scarce breath to speak with; and upon that he gave me the key of the spirit locker, and I began to go slowly back to the round-house. What was I to do? They were dogs and thieves; they had stolen me from my own country; they had killed poor Ransome; and was I to hold the candle to another murder? But then, upon the other hand, there was the fear of death very plain before me; for what could a boy and a man, if they were as brave as lions, against a whole ship's company?

I was still arguing it back and forth, and getting no great clearness, when I came into the round-house and saw the Jacobite eating his supper under the lamp; and at that my mind was made up all in a moment. I have no credit by it; it was by no choice of mine, but as if by compulsion, that I walked right up to the table and put my hand on his shoulder.

"Do ye want to be killed?" said I. He sprang to his feet, and looked a question at me as clear as if he had spoken.

"O!" cried I, "they're all murderers here; it's a ship full of them! They've murdered a boy already. Now it's you."

"Ay, ay," said he; "but they haven't got me yet." And then looking at me curiously, "Will ye stand with me?"

"That will I!" said I. "I am no thief, nor yet murderer. I'll stand by you."

"Why, then," said he, "what's your name?"

"David Balfour," said I; and then, thinking that a man with so fine a coat must like fine people, I added for the first time, "of Shaws."

It never occurred to him to doubt me, for a Highlander is used to see great gentlefolk in great poverty; but as he had no estate of his own, my words nettled a very childish vanity he had.

"My name is Stewart," he said, drawing himself up. "Alan Breck, they call me. A king's name is good enough for me, though I bear it plain and have the name of no farm-midden to clap to the hind-end of it."

And having administered this rebuke, as though it were something of a chief importance, he turned to examine our defences.

The round-house was built very strong, to support the breaching of the seas. Of its five apertures, only the skylight and the two doors were large enough for the passage of a man. The doors, besides, could be drawn close: They were of stout oak, and ran in grooves, and were fitted with hooks to keep them either shut or open, as the need arose. The one that was already shut I secured in this fashion; but when I was proceeding to slide to the other, Alan stopped me.

"David," said he, "—for I cannae bring to mind the name of your landed estate, and so will make so bold as to call you David—that door, being open, is the best part of my defences."

"It would be yet better shut," says I.

"Not so, David," says he. "Ye see, I have but one face; but so long as that door is open and my face to it, the best part of my enemies will be in front of me, where I would aye wish to find them."

Then he gave me from the rack a cutlass (of which there were a few besides the firearms), choosing it with great care, shaking his head and saying he had never in all his life seen poorer weapons; and next he set me down to the table with a powder-horn, a bag of bullets and all the pistols, which he bade me charge.

"And that will be better work, let me tell you," said he, "for a gentleman of decent birth, than scraping plates and reachin' drams to a wheen tarry sailors."

Thereupon he stood up in the midst with his face to the door and, drawing his great sword, made trial of the room he had to wield it in.

"I must stick to the point," he said, shaking his head; "and that's a pity, too. It doesn't set my genius, which is all for the upper guard. And, now," said he, "do you keep on charging the pistols, and give heed to me."

I told him I would listen closely. My chest was tight, my mouth dry, the light dark to my eyes; the thought of the numbers that were soon to leap in upon us kept my heart in a flutter; and the sea, which I heard washing round the brig, and where I thought my dead body would be cast ere morning, ran in my mind strangely.

"First of all," said he, "how many are against us?"

I reckoned them up; and such was the hurry of my mind, I had to cast the numbers twice. "Fifteen," said I.

Alan whistled. "Well," said he, "that can't be cured. And now follow me. It is my part to keep this door, where I look for the main battle. In that, ye have no hand. And mind and dinnae fire to this side unless they get me down; for I would rather have ten foes in front of me than one friend like you cracking pistols at my back."

I told him, indeed, I was no great shot.

"And that's very bravely said," he cried, in a great admiration of my candour. "There's many a pretty gentleman that would nae dare to say it."

"But then, sir," said I, "there is the door behind you, which they may perhaps break in."

"Ay," said he, "and that is a part of your work. No sooner the pistols charged, than ye must climb up into yon bed where ye're handy at the window; and if they lift hand against the door, ye're to shoot. But that's not all. Let's make a bit of a soldier of ye, David. What else have ye to guard?"

"There's the skylight," said I. "But indeed, Mr. Stewart, I would need to have eyes upon both sides to keep the two of them; for when my face is at the one, my back is to the other."

"And that's very true," said Alan. "But have ye no ears to your head?"

"To be sure!" cried I. "I must hear the bursting of the glass!"

"Ye have some rudiments of sense," said Alan, grimly.

But now our time of truce was come to an end. Those on deck had waited for my coming till they grew impatient; and scarce had Alan spoken, when the captain showed face in the open door.

"Stand!" cried Alan, and pointed his sword at him. The captain stood, indeed; but he neither winced nor drew back a foot.

"A naked sword?" says he. "This is a strange return for hospitality."

"Do ye see me?" said Alan. "I am come of kings; I bear a king's name. My badge is the oak. Do ye see my sword? It has slashed the heads off mair Whigamores than you have toes upon your feet. Call up your vermin to your back, sir, and fall on! The sooner the clash begins, the sooner ye'll taste this steel throughout your vitals."

The captain said nothing to Alan, but he looked over at me with an ugly look. "David," said he, "I'll mind this;" and the sound of his voice went through me with a jar.

Next moment he was gone.

"And now," said Alan, "let your hand keep your head, for the grip is coming."

Alan drew a dirk, which he held in his left hand in case they should run in under his sword. I, on my part, clambered up into the berth with an armful of pistols and something of a heavy heart, and set open the window where I was to watch. It was a small part of the deck that I could overlook, but enough for our purpose. The sea had gone down, and the wind was steady and kept the sails quiet; so that there was a great stillness in the ship, in which I made sure I heard the sound of muttering voices. A little after, and there came a clash of steel upon the deck, by which I knew they were dealing out the cutlasses and one had been let fall; and after that, silence again.

I do not know if I was what you call afraid; but my heart beat like a bird's, both quick and little; and there was a dimness came before my eyes which I continually rubbed away, and which continually returned. As for hope, I had none; but only a darkness of despair and a sort of anger against all the world that made me long to sell my life as dear as I was able. I tried to pray, I remember, but that same hurry of my mind, like a man running, would not suffer me to think upon the words; and my chief wish was to have the thing begin and be done with it.

It came all of a sudden when it did, with a rush of feet and a roar, and then a shout from Alan, and a sound of blows and some one crying out as if hurt. I looked back over my shoulder, and saw Mr. Shuan in the doorway, crossing blades with Alan.

"That's him that killed the boy!" I cried.

"Look to your window!" said Alan; and as I turned back to my place, I saw him pass his sword through the mate's body.

It was none too soon for me to look to my own part; for my head was scarce back at the window, before five men, carrying a spare yard for a battering-ram, ran past me and took post to drive the door in. I had never fired with a pistol in my life, and not often with a gun; far less against a fellow-creature. But it was now or never; and just as they swang the yard, I cried out: "Take that!" and shot into their midst.

I must have hit one of them, for he sang out and gave back a step, and the rest stopped as if a little disconcerted. Before they had time to recover, I sent another ball over their heads; and at my third shot (which went as wide as the second) the whole party threw down the yard and ran for it.

Then I looked round again into the deck-house. The whole place was full of the smoke of my own firing, just as my ears seemed to be burst with the noise of the shots. But there was Alan, standing as before; only now his sword was running blood to the hilt, and himself so swelled with triumph and fallen into so fine an attitude that he looked to be invincible. Right before him on the floor was Mr. Shuan, on his hands and knees; the blood was pouring from his mouth, and he was sinking slowly lower, with a terrible, white face; and just as I looked, some of those from behind caught hold of him by the heels and dragged him bodily out of the round-house. I believe he died as they were doing it.

"There's one of your Whigs for ye!" cried Alan; and then, turning to me, he asked if I had done much execution.

I told him I had winged one, and thought it was the captain.

"And I've settled two," says he. "No, there's not enough blood let; they'll be back again. To your watch, David. This was but a dram before meat."

I settled back to my place, re-charging the three pistols I had fired, and keeping watch with both eye and ear.

Our enemies were disputing not far off upon the deck, and that so loudly that I could hear a word or two above the washing of the seas.

"It was Shuan bungled it," I heard one say.

And another answered him with a "Wheesht, man! He's paid the piper."

After that the voices fell again into the same muttering as before. Only now, one person spoke most of the time, as though laying down a plan, and first one and then another answered him briefly, like men taking orders. By this, I made sure they were coming on again, and told Alan.

"It's what we have to pray for," said he. "Unless we can give them a good distaste of us, and done with it, there'll be nae sleep for either you or me. But this time, mind, they'll be in earnest."

By this, my pistols were ready, and there was nothing to do but listen and wait. While the brush lasted, I had not the time to think if I was frighted; but now, when all was still again, my mind ran upon nothing else. The thought of the sharp swords and the cold steel was strong in me; and presently, when I began to hear stealthy steps and a brushing of men's clothes against the round-house wall, and knew they were taking their places in the dark, I could have found it in my mind to cry out aloud.

All this was upon Alan's side; and I had begun to think my share of the fight was at an end, when I heard someone drop softly on the roof above me.

Then there came a single call on the sea-pipe, and that was the signal. A knot of them made one rush of it, cutlass in hand, against the door; and at the same moment, the glass of the skylight was dashed in a thousand pieces, and a man leaped through and landed on the floor. Before he got his feet, I had clapped a pistol to his back, and might have shot him, too; only at the touch of him (and him alive) my whole flesh misgave me, and I could no more pull the trigger than I could have flown.

He had dropped his cutlass as he jumped, and when he felt the pistol, whipped straight round and laid hold of me, roaring out an oath; and at that either my courage came again, or I grew so much afraid as came to the same thing; for I gave a shriek and shot him in the midst of the body. He gave the most horrible, ugly groan and fell to the floor. The foot of a second fellow, whose legs were dangling through the skylight, struck me at the same time upon the head; and at that I snatched another pistol and shot this one through the thigh, so that he slipped through and tumbled in a lump on his companion's body. There was no talk of missing, any more than there was time to aim; I clapped the muzzle to the very place and fired.

I might have stood and stared at them for long, but I heard Alan shout as if for help, and that brought me to my senses.

He had kept the door so long; but one of the seamen, while he was engaged with others, had run in under his guard and caught him about the body. Alan was dirking him with his left hand, but the fellow clung like a leech. Another had broken in and had his cutlass raised. The door was thronged with their faces. I thought we were lost, and catching up my cutlass, fell on them in flank.

But I had not time to be of help. The wrestler dropped at last; and Alan, leaping back to get his distance, ran upon the others like a bull, roaring as he went. They broke before him like water, turning, and running, and falling one against another in their haste. The sword in his hands flashed like quicksilver into the huddle of our fleeing enemies; and at every flash there came the scream of a man hurt. I was still thinking we were lost when lo! they were all gone, and Alan was driving them along the deck as a sheep-dog chases sheep.

Yet he was no sooner out than he was back again, being as cautious as he was brave; and meanwhile the seamen continued running and crying out as if he was still behind them; and we heard them tumble one upon another into the forecastle, and clap-to the hatch upon the top.

The round-house was like a shambles; three were dead inside, another lay in his death agony across the threshold; and there were Alan and I victorious and unhurt.

He came up to me with open arms. "Come to my arms!" he cried, and embraced and kissed me hard upon both cheeks. "David," said he, "I love you like a brother. And O, man," he cried in a kind of ecstasy, "am I no a bonny fighter?"

Thereupon he turned to the four enemies, passed his sword clean through each of them, and tumbled them out of doors one after the other. As he did so, he kept humming and singing and whistling to himself, like a man trying to recall an air; only what *he* was trying was to make one. All the while, the flush was in his face, and his eyes were as bright as a five-year-old child's with a new toy. And presently he sat down upon the table, sword in hand; the air that he was making all the time began to run a little clearer, and then clearer still; and then out he burst with a great voice into a Gaelic song.

I have translated it here, not in verse (of which I have no skill) but at least in the king's English.

He sang it often afterwards, and the thing became popular; so that I have heard it and had it explained to me, many's the time.

*This is the song of the sword of Alan;*
*The smith made it,*
*The fire set it;*
*Now it shines in the hand of Alan Breck.*

*Their eyes were many and bright,*
*Swift were they to behold,*
*Many the hands they guided:*
*The sword was alone*

*The dun deer troop over the hill,*
*They are many, the hill is one;*
*The dun deer vanish,*
*The hill remains.*

*Come to me from the hills of heather,*
*Come from the isles of the sea.*
*O far-beholding eagles,*
*Here is your meat.*

Now this song, which he made (both words and music) in the hour of our victory, is something less than just to me, who stood beside him in the tussle. Mr. Shuan and five more were either killed outright or thoroughly disabled; but of these, two fell by my hand, the two that came by the skylight. Four more were hurt, and of that number, one (and he not the least important) got his hurt from me. So that, altogether, I did my fair share both of the killing and the wounding, and might have claimed a place in Alan's verses. But poets have to think upon their rhymes; and in good prose talk, Alan always did me more than justice.

In the meanwhile, I was innocent of any wrong being done me. For not only I knew no word of the Gaelic; but what with the long suspense of the waiting, and the scurry and strain of our two spirts of fighting, and more than all, the horror I had of some of my own share in it, the thing was no sooner over than I was glad to stagger to a seat. There was that tightness on my chest that I could hardly breathe; the thought of the two men I had shot sat upon me like a nightmare; and all upon a sudden, and before I had a guess of what was coming, I began to sob and cry like any child.

Alan clapped my shoulder, and said I was a brave lad and wanted nothing but a sleep.

"I'll take the first watch," said he. "Ye've done well by me, David, first and last; and I wouldn't lose you for all Appin—no, nor for Breadalbane."

So I made up my bed on the floor; and he took the first spell, pistol in hand and sword on knee, three hours by the captain's watch upon the wall. Then he roused me up, and I took my turn of three hours; before the end of which it was broad day, and a very quiet morning, with a smooth, rolling sea that

# Captain Sharkey

## *Arthur Conan Doyle*

When the great wars of the Spanish Succession had been brought to an end by the Treaty of Utrecht, the vast number of privateers which had been fitted out by the contending parties found their occupation gone. Some took to the more peaceful but less lucrative ways of ordinary commerce, others were absorbed into the fishing-fleets, and a few of the more reckless hoisted the Jolly Roger at the mizzen and the bloody flag at the main, declaring a private war upon their own account against the whole human race.

With mixed crews, recruited from every nation, they scoured the seas, disappearing occasionally to careen in some lonely inlet, or putting in for a debauch at some outlying port, where they dazzled the inhabitants by their lavishness and horrified them by their brutalities.

On the Coromandel Coast, at Madagascar, in the African waters, and above all in the West Indian and American seas, the pirates were a constant menace: With an insolent luxury they would regulate their depredations by the comfort of the seasons, harrying New England in the summer and dropping south again to the tropical islands in the winter.

They were the more to be dreaded because they had none of that discipline and restraint which made their predecessors, the Buccaneers, both formidable and respectable. These Ishmaels of the sea rendered an account to no man, and treated their prisoners according to the drunken whim of the moment. Flashes of grotesque generosity alternated with longer stretches of inconceivable ferocity, and the skipper who fell into their hands might find himself dismissed with his cargo, after serving as boon companion in some hideous debauch, or might sit at his cabin table with his own nose and his lips served up with pepper and salt in front of him. It took a stout seaman in those days to ply his calling in the Caribbean Gulf.

Such a man was Captain John Scarrow, of the ship *Morning Star*, and yet he breathed a long sigh of relief when he heard the splash of the falling anchor and swung at his moorings within a hundred yards of the guns of the citadel of Basseterre. St. Kitt's was his final port of call, and early next morning his bowsprit would be pointed for Old England. He had had enough of those robber-haunted seas. Ever since he had left Maracaibo upon the Main, with his full lading of sugar and red pepper, he had winced at every topsail which glimmered over the violet edge of the tropical sea. He had coasted up the Windward Islands, touching here and there, and assailed continually by stories of villainy and outrage.

Captain Sharkey, of the 20-gun pirate barque *Happy Delivery*, had passed down the coast, and had littered it with gutted vessels and with murdered men. Dreadful anecdotes were current of his grim pleasantries and of his inflexible ferocity. From the Bahamas to the Main his coal-black barque, with the ambiguous name, had been freighted with death and many things which are worse than death. So nervous was Captain Scarrow, with his new full-rigged ship and her full and valuable lading, that he struck out to the west as far as Bird's Island to be out of the usual track of commerce. And yet even in those solitary waters he had been unable to shake off sinister traces of Captain Sharkey.

One morning they had raised a single skiff adrift upon the face of the ocean. Its only occupant was a delirious seaman, who yelled hoarsely as they hoisted him aboard, and showed a dried-up tongue like a black and wrinkled fungus at the back of his mouth. Water and nursing soon transformed him into the strongest and smartest sailor on the ship. He was from Marblehead, in New England, it seemed, and was the sole survivor of a schooner which had been scuttled by the dreadful Sharkey.

For a week Hiram Evanson, for that was his name, had been adrift beneath a tropical sun. Sharkey had ordered the mangled remains of his late captain to be thrown into the boat, "as provisions for the voyage," but the seaman had at once committed them to the deep, lest the temptation should be more than he could bear. He had lived upon his own huge frame, until, at the last moment, the *Morning Star* had found him in that madness which is the precursor of such a death. It was no bad find for Captain Scarrow, for, with a short-handed crew, such a seaman as this big New Englander was a prize worth having. He vowed that he was the only man whom Captain Sharkey had ever placed under an obligation.

Now that they lay under the guns of Basseterre, all danger from the pirate was at an end, and yet the thought of him lay heavily upon the seaman's mind as he watched the agent's boat shooting out from the custom-house quay.

"I'll lay you a wager, Morgan," said he to the first mate, "that the agent will speak of Sharkey in the first hundred words that pass his lips."

"Well, captain, I'll have you a silver dollar, and chance it," said the rough old Bristol man beside him.

The rowers shot the boat alongside, and the linen-clad steersman sprang up the ladder.

"Welcome, Captain Scarrow!" he cried. "Have you heard about Sharkey?"

The captain grinned at the mate.

"What devilry has he been up to now?" he asked.

"Devilry! You've not heard, then! Why, we've got him safe under lock and key here at Basseterre. He was tried last Wednesday, and he is to be hanged tomorrow morning."

Captain and mate gave a shout of joy, which an instant later was taken up by the crew. Discipline was forgotten as they scrambled up through the break of the poop to hear the news. The New Englander was in the front of them with a radiant face turned up to heaven, for he came of the Puritan stock.

"Sharkey to be hanged," he cried. "You don't know, Master Agent, if they lack a hangman, do you?"

"Stand back!" cried the mate, whose outraged sense of discipline was even stronger than his interest at the news. "I'll pay that dollar, Captain Scarrow, with the lightest heart that ever I paid a wager yet. How came the villain to be taken?"

"Why, as to that, he became more than his own comrades could abide, and they took such a horror of him that they would not have him on the ship. So they marooned him upon the Little Mangles to the south of the Mysteriosa Bank, and there he was found by a Portobello trader, who brought him in. There was talk of sending him to Jamaica to be tried, but our good little governor, Sir Charles Ewan, would not hear of it. 'He's my meat,' said he, 'and I claim the cooking of it.' If you can stay till to-morrow morning at ten, you'll see the joint swinging."

"I wish I could," said the captain, wistfully, "but I am sadly behind time now. I should start with the evening tide."

"That you can't do," said the agent with decision. "The Governor is going back with you."

"The Governor!"

"Yes. He's had a dispatch from Government to return without delay. The fly-boat that brought it has gone on to Virginia. So Sir Charles has been waiting for you, as I told him you were due before the rains."

"Well, well!" cried the captain, in some perplexity, "I'm a plain seaman, and I don't know much of governors and baronets and their ways. I don't remember that I ever so much as spoke to one. But if it's in King George's service, and he asks a cast in the *Morning Star* as far as London, I'll do what I can for him. There's my own cabin he can have and welcome. As to the cooking, it's lobscouse and salmagundy six days in the week; but he can bring his own cook aboard with him if he thinks our galley too rough for his taste."

"You need not trouble your mind, Captain Scarrow," said the agent. "Sir Charles is in weak health just now, only clear of a quartan ague, and it is likely he will keep his cabin most of the voyage. Dr. Larousse said that he would have sunk had the hanging of Sharkey not put fresh life into him. He has a great spirit in him, though, and you must not blame him if he is somewhat short in his speech."

"He may say what he likes and do what he likes so long as he does not come athwart my hawse when I am working the ship," said the captain. "He is Governor of St. Kitt's, but I am Governor of the *Morning Star*. And, by his leave, I must weigh with the first tide, for I owe a duty to my employer, just as he does to King George."

"He can scarce be ready to-night, for he has many things to set in order before he leaves."

"The early morning tide, then."

"Very good. I shall send his things aboard to-night, and he will follow them to-morrow early if I can prevail upon him to leave St. Kitt's without seeing Sharkey do the rogue's hornpipe. His own orders were instant, so it may be that he will come at once. It is likely that Dr. Larousse may attend him upon the journey."

Left to themselves, the captain and mate made the best preparations which they could for their illustrious passenger. The largest cabin was turned out and adorned in his honour, and orders were given by which barrels of fruit and some cases of wine should be brought off to vary the plain food of an ocean-going trader. In the evening the Governor's baggage began to arrive—great ironbound ant-proof trunks, and official tin packing-cases, with other strange-shaped packages, which suggested the cocked hat or the sword within. And then there came a note, with a heraldic device upon the big red seal, to say that Sir Charles Ewan made his compliments to Captain Scarrow, and that he hoped to be with him in the morning as early as his duties and his infirmities would permit.

He was as good as his word, for the first grey of dawn had hardly begun to deepen into pink when he was brought alongside, and climbed with some difficulty up the ladder. The captain had heard that the Governor was an eccentric, but he was hardly prepared for the curious figure who came limping feebly down his quarterdeck, his steps supported by a thick bamboo cane. He wore a Ramillies wig, all twisted into little tails like a poodle's coat, and cut so low across the brow that the large green glasses which covered his eyes looked as if they were hung from it. A fierce beak of a nose, very long and very thin, cut the air in front of him. His ague had caused him to swathe his throat and chin with a broad linen cravat, and he wore a loose damask powdering-gown secured by a cord round the waist. As he advanced he carried his masterful nose high in the air, but his head turned slowly from side to side in the helpless manner of the purblind, and he called in a high, querulous voice for the captain.

"You have my things?" he asked.

"Yes, Sir Charles."

"Have you wine aboard?"

"I have ordered five cases, sir."

"And tobacco."

"There is a keg of Trinidad."

"You play a hand at piquet?"

"Passably well, sir."

"Then up anchor, and to sea!"

There was a fresh westerly wind, so by the time the sun was fairly through the morning haze, the ship was hull down from the islands. The decrepit Governor still limped the deck, with one guiding hand upon the quarter-rail.

"You are on Government service now, captain," said he. "They are counting the days till I come to Westminster, I promise you. Have you all that she will carry?"

"Every inch, Sir Charles?"

"Keep her so if you blow the sails out of her. I fear, Captain Scarrow, that you will find a blind and broken man a poor companion for your voyage."

"I am honoured in enjoying your Excellency's society," said the captain. "But I am sorry that your eyes should be so afflicted."

"Yes, indeed. It is the cursed glare of the sun on the white streets of Basseterre which has gone far to burn them out."

"I had heard also that you had been plagued by a quartan ague."

"Yes; I have had a pyrexy, which has reduced me much."

"We had set aside a cabin for your surgeon."

"Ah, the rascal! There was no budging him, for he has a snug business amongst the merchants. But hark!"

He raised his ring-covered hand in the air. From far astern there came the low deep thunder of cannon.

"It is from the island!!" cried the captain in astonishment. "Can it be a signal for us to put back?" The Governor laughed.

"You have heard that Sharkey, the pirate, is to be hanged this morning. I ordered the batteries to salute when the rascal was kicking his last, so that I might know of it out at sea. There's an end of Sharkey!"

"There's an end of Sharkey!" cried the captain; and the crew took up the cry as they gathered in little knots upon the deck and stared back at the low, purple line of the vanishing land.

It was a cheering omen for their start across the Western Ocean, and the invalid Governor found himself a popular man on board, for it was generally understood that but for his insistence upon an immediate trial and sentence, the villain might have played upon some more venal judge and so escaped. At dinner that day Sir Charles gave many anecdotes of the deceased pirate; and so affable was he, and so skilful in adapting his conversation to men of lower degree, that captain, mate, and Governor smoked their long pipes and drank their claret as three good comrades should.

"And what figure did Sharkey cut in the dock?" asked the captain.

"He is a man of some presence," said the Governor.

"I had always understood that he was an ugly, sneering devil," remarked the mate.

"Well, I dare say he could look ugly upon occasions," said the Governor.

"I have heard a New Bedford whaleman say that he could not forget his eyes," said Captain Scarrow. "They were of the lightest filmy blue, with red-rimmed lids. Was that not so, Sir Charles?"

"Alas, my own eyes will not permit me to know much of those of others! But I remember now that the Adjutant-General said that he had such an eye as you describe, and added that the jury were so foolish as to be visibly discomposed when it was turned upon them. It is well for them that he is dead, for he was a man who would never forget an injury, and if he had laid hands upon any one of them he would have stuffed him with straw and hung him for a figure-head."

The idea seemed to amuse the Governor, for he broke suddenly into a high, neighing laugh, and the two seamen laughed also, but not so heartily, for they remembered that Sharkey was not the last pirate who sailed the western seas, and that as grotesque a fate might come to be their own. Another bottle was broached to drink to a pleasant voyage, and the Governor would drink just one other on the top of it, so that the seamen were glad at last to stagger off—the one to his watch and the other to his bunk. But when, after his four hours' spell, the mate came down again, he was amazed to see the Governor in his Ramillies wig, his glasses, and his powdering-gown still seated sedately at the lonely table with his reeking pipe and six black bottles by his side.

"I have drunk with the Governor of St. Kitt's when he was sick," said he, "and God forbid that I should ever try to keep pace with him when he is well."

The voyage of the *Morning Star* was a successful one, and in about three weeks she was at the mouth of the British Channel.

From the first day the infirm Governor had begun to recover his strength, and before they were halfway across the Atlantic he was, save only for his eyes, as well as any man upon the ship. Those who uphold the nourishing qualities of wine might point to him in triumph, for never a night passed that he did not repeat the performance of his first one. And yet he would be out upon deck in the early morning as fresh and brisk as the best of them, peering about with his weak eyes, and asking questions about the sails and the rigging, for he was anxious to learn the ways of the sea. And he made up for the deficiency of his eyes by obtaining leave from the captain that the New England seaman—he who had been cast away in the boat—should lead him about, and above all that he should sit beside him when he played cards and count the number of the pips, for unaided he could not tell the king from the knave.

It was natural that this Evanson should do the Governor willing service, since the one was the victim of the vile Sharkey, and the other was his avenger. One could see that it was a pleasure to the big American to lend his arm to the invalid, and at night he would stand with all respect behind his chair in the cabin and lay his great stub-nailed forefinger upon the card which he should play. Between them there was little in the pockets either of Captain Scarrow or of Morgan, the first mate, by the time they sighted the Lizard.

And it was not long before they found that all they had heard of the high temper of Sir Charles Ewan fell short of the mark. At a sign of opposition or a word of argument his chin would shoot out from his cravat, his masterful nose would be cocked at a higher and more insolent angle, and his bamboo cane would whistle up over his shoulder. He cracked it once over the head of the carpenter when the man had accidentally jostled him upon the deck. Once, too, when there was some grumbling and talk of a mutiny over the state of the provisions; he was of opinion that they should not wait for the dogs to rise, but that they should march forward and set upon them until they had trounced the devilment out of them. "Give me a knife and a bucket!" he cried with an oath, and could hardly be withheld from setting forth alone to deal with the spokesman of the seamen.

Captain Scarrow had to remind him that though he might be only answerable to himself at St. Kitt's, killing became murder upon the high seas. In politics he was, as became his official position, a stout prop of the House of Hanover, and he swore in his cups that he had never met a Jacobite without pistolling him where he stood. Yet for all his vapouring and his violence he was so good a companion, with such a stream of strange anecdote and reminiscence, that Scarrow and Morgan had never known a voyage pass so pleasantly.

And then at length came the last day, when, after passing the island, they had struck land again at the high white cliffs at Beachy Head. As evening fell the ship lay rolling in an oily calm, a league off from Winchelsea, with the long dark snout of Dungeness jutting out in front of her. Next morning they would pick up their pilot at the Foreland, and Sir Charles might meet the king's ministers at Westminster before the evening. The boatswain had the watch, and the three friends were met for a last turn of cards in the cabin, the faithful American still serving as eyes to the Governor. There was a good stake upon the table, for the sailors had tried on this last night to win their losses back from their passenger. Suddenly he threw his cards down, and swept all the money into the pocket of his long-flapped silken waistcoat.

"The game's mine!" said he.

"Heh, Sir Charles, not so fast!" cried Captain Scarrow; "you have not played out the hand, and we are not the losers."

"Sink you for a liar!" said the Governor. "I tell you that I have played out the hand, and that you are a loser." He whipped off his wig and his glasses as he spoke, and there was a high, bald forehead, and a pair of shifty blue eyes with the red rims of a bull terrier.

"Good God!" cried the mate. "It's Sharkey!"

The two sailors sprang from their seats, but the big American castaway had put his huge back against the cabin door, and he held a pistol in each of his hands. The passenger had also laid a pistol upon the scattered cards in front of him, and he burst into his high, neighing laugh.

"Captain Sharkey is the name, gentlemen," said he, "and this is Roaring Ned Galloway, the quartermaster of the *Happy Delivery*. We made it hot, and so they marooned us: me on a dry Tortuga cay, and him in an oarless boat. You dogs—you poor, fond, water-hearted dogs—we hold you at the end of our pistols!"

"You may shoot, or you may not!" cried Scarrow, striking his hand upon the breast of his frieze jacket. "If it's my last breath, Sharkey, I tell you that you are a bloody rogue and miscreant, with a halter and hell-fire in store for you."

"There's a man of spirit, and one of my own kidney, and he's going to make a very pretty death of it!" cried Sharkey. "There's no one aft save the man at the wheel, so you may keep your breath, for you'll need it soon. Is the dinghy astern, Ned?"

"Ay, ay, captain!"

"And the other boats scuttled?"

"I bored them all in three places."

"Then we shall have to leave you, Captain Scarrow. You look as if you hadn't quite got your bearings yet. Is there anything you'd like to ask me?"

"I believe you're the devil himself!" cried the captain. "Where is the Governor of St. Kitt's?"

"When last I saw him his Excellency was in bed with his throat cut. When I broke prison I learnt from my friends—for Captain Sharkey has those who love him in every port—that the Governor was starting for Europe under a master who had never seen him. I climbed his verandah and I paid him the little debt that I owed him. Then I came aboard you with such of his things as I had need of, and a pair of glasses to hide these tell-tale eyes of mine, and I have ruffled it as a governor should. Now, Ned, you can get to work upon them."

"Help! Help! Watch ahoy!" yelled the mate; but the butt of the pirate's pistol crashed down on to his head, and he dropped like a pithed ox. Scarrow rushed for the door, but the sentinel clapped his hand over his mouth, and threw his other arm round his waist.

"No use, Master Scarrow," said Sharkey. "Let us see you go down on your knees and beg for your life."

"I'll see you—" cried Scarrow, shaking his mouth clear.

"Twist his arm round, Ned. Now will you?"

"No; not if you twist it off."

"Put an inch of your knife into him."

"You may put six inches, and then I won't."

"Sink me, but I like his spirit!" cried Sharkey. "Put your knife in your pocket, Ned. You've saved your skin, Scarrow, and it's a pity so stout a man should not take to the only trade where a pretty fellow can pick up a living. You must be born for no common death, Scarrow, since you have lain at my mercy and lived to tell the story. Tie him up, Ned."

"To the stove, captain?"

"Tut, tut! There's a fire in the stove. None of your rover tricks, Ned Galloway, unless they are called for, or I'll let you know which of us two is captain and which is quartermaster. Make him fast to the table."

"Nay, I thought you meant to roast him!" said the quartermaster. "You surely do not mean to let him go?"

"If you and I were marooned on a Bahama cay, Ned Galloway, it is still for me to command and for you to obey. Sink you for a villain, do you dare to question my orders?"

"Nay, nay, Captain Sharkey, not so hot, sir!" said the quartermaster, and, lifting Scarrow like a child, he laid him on the table. With the quick dexterity of a seaman, he tied his spreadeagled hands and feet with a rope which was passed underneath, and gagged him securely with the long cravat which used to adorn the chin of the Governor of St. Kitt's.

"Now, Captain Scarrow, we must take our leave of you," said the pirate. "If I had half a dozen of my brisk boys at my heels

I should have had your cargo and your ship, but Roaring Ned could not find a foremast hand with the spirit of a mouse. I see there are some small craft about, and we shall get one of them. When Captain Sharkey has a boat he can get a smack, when he has a smack he can get a brig, when he has a brig he can get a barque, and when he has a barque he'll soon have a full-rigged ship of his own—so make haste into London town, or I may be coming back, after all, for the *Morning Star*."

Captain Scarrow heard the key turn in the lock as they left the cabin. Then, as he strained at his bonds, he heard their footsteps pass up the companion and along the quarterdeck to where the dinghy hung in the stern. Then, still struggling and writhing, he heard the creak of the falls and the splash of the boat in the water. In a mad fury he tore and dragged at his ropes, until at last, with flayed wrists and ankles, he rolled from the table, sprang over the dead mate, kicked his way through the closed door, and rushed hatless on to the deck.

"Ahoy! Peterson, Armitage, Wilson!" he screamed. "Cutlasses and pistols! Clear away the long-boat! Clear away the gig! Sharkey, the pirate, is in yonder dinghy. Whistle up the larboard watch, bo'sun, and tumble into the boats all hands."

Down splashed the long-boat and down splashed the gig, but in an instant the coxswains and crews were swarming up the falls on to the deck once more.

"The boats are scuttled!" they cried. "They are leaking like a sieve."

The captain gave a bitter curse. He had been beaten and outwitted at every point. Above was a cloudless, starlit sky, with neither wind nor the promise of it. The sails flapped idly in the moonlight. Far away lay a fishing-smack, with the men clustering over their net.

Close to them was the little dinghy, dipping and lifting over the shining swell.

"They are dead men!" cried the captain. "A shout all together, boys, to warn them of their danger."

But it was too late.

At that very moment the dinghy shot into the shadow of the fishing-boat. There were two rapid pistol-shots, a scream, and then another pistol-shot, followed by silence. The clustering fishermen had disappeared. And then, suddenly, as the first puffs of a land-breeze came out from the Sussex shore, the boom swung out, the mainsail filled, and the little craft crept out with her nose to the Atlantic.

# A Thief and a Pirate

## *Rafael Sabatini*

Captain Blood paced the poop of his ship alone in the tepid dusk and the growing golden radiance of the great poop lantern in which a seaman had just lighted the three lamps. About him all was peace.

The signs of the day's battle had been effaced, the decks had been swabbed, and order was restored above and below. A group of men squatting about the main hatch were drowsily chanting, their hardened natures softened, perhaps, by the calm and beauty of the night. They were the men of the larboard watch, waiting for eight bells which was imminent.

Captain Blood did not hear them; he did not hear anything save the echo of those cruel words which had dubbed him thief and pirate.

Thief and pirate!

It is an odd fact of human nature that a man may for years possess the knowledge that a certain thing must be of a certain fashion, and yet be shocked to discover through his own senses that the fact is in perfect harmony with his beliefs. When first, three years ago, at Tortuga he had been urged upon the adventurer's course which he had followed ever since, he had known in what opinion Arabella Bishop must hold him if he succumbed. Only the conviction that already she was for ever lost to him, by introducing a certain desperate recklessness into his soul, had supplied the final impulse to drive him upon his rover's course.

That he should ever meet her again had not entered his calculations, had found no place in his dreams. They were, he conceived, irrevocably and for ever parted. Yet, in spite of this, in spite even of the persuasion that to her this reflection that was his torment could bring no regrets, he had kept the thought of her ever before him in all those wild years of filibustering. He had used it as a curb not only upon himself, but also upon those who followed him. Never had buccaneers been so rigidly held in hand, never had they been so firmly restrained, never so debarred from the excesses of rapine and lust that were usual in their kind, as those who sailed with Captain Blood. It was, you will remember, stipulated in their articles that in these, as in other matters, they must submit to the commands of their leader. And because of the singular good fortune which had attended his leadership, he had been able to impose that stern condition of a discipline unknown before among buccaneers.

How would not these men laugh at him now if he were to tell them that this he had done out of respect for a slip of a girl of whom he had fallen romantically enamoured? How would not that laughter swell if he added that this girl had that day informed him that she did not number thieves and pirates among her acquaintance.

Thief and pirate!

How the words clung, how they stung and burnt his brain!

It did not occur to him, being no psychologist, nor learned in the tortuous workings of the feminine mind, that the fact that she should bestow upon him those epithets in the very moment and circumstance of their meeting was in itself curious. He did not perceive the problem thus presented; therefore he could not probe it. Else he might have concluded that, if in a moment in which by delivering her from captivity he deserved her gratitude, yet she expressed herself in bitterness, it must be because that bitterness was anterior to the gratitude and deep-seated. She had been moved to it by hearing of the course he had taken. Why? It was what he did not ask himself, or some ray of light might have come to brighten his dark, his utterly evil despondency. Surely she would never have been so moved had she not cared—had she not felt that in what he did there was a personal wrong to herself. Surely, he might have reasoned, nothing short of this could have moved her to such a degree of bitterness and scorn as that which she had displayed.

That is how you will reason. Not so, however, reasoned Captain Blood. Indeed, that night he reasoned not at all. His soul was given up to conflict between the almost sacred love he had borne her in all these years and the evil passion which she had now awakened in him. Extremes touch, and in touching may for a space become confused, indistinguishable. And the extremes of love and hate were to-night so confused in the soul of Captain Blood that in their fusion they made up a monstrous passion.

Thief and pirate!

That was what she deemed him, without qualification, oblivious of the deep wrongs he had suffered, the desperate case in which he found himself after his escape from Barbados, and all the rest that had gone to make him what he was. That he should have conducted his filibustering with hands as clean as were possible to a man engaged in such undertakings had also not occurred to her as a charitable thought with which to mitigate her judgment of a man she had once esteemed. She had no charity for him, no mercy. She had summed him up, convicted him and sentenced him in that one phrase. He was thief and pirate in her eyes; nothing more, nothing less. What, then, was she? What are those who have no charity? He asked the stars. Well, as she had shaped him hitherto, so let her shape him now. Thief and pirate she had branded him. She should be justified. Thief and pirate should he prove henceforth; no more nor less; as bowelless, as remorseless as all those others who had deserved those names. He would cast out the maudlin ideals by which he had sought to steer a course; put an end to this idiotic struggle to make the best of two worlds. She had shown him clearly to which world he belonged. Let him now justify her. She was aboard his ship, in his power, and he desired her.

He laughed softly, jeeringly, as he leaned on the taffrail, looking down at the phosphorescent gleam in the ship's wake, and his own laughter startled him by its evil note. He checked suddenly, and shivered. A sob broke from him to end that ribald burst of mirth. He took his face in his hands and found a chill moisture on his brow. Meanwhile, Lord Julian, who knew the feminine part of humanity rather better than Captain Blood, was engaged in solving the curious problem that had so completely escaped the buccaneer. He was spurred to it, I suspect, by certain vague stirrings of jealousy. Miss Bishop's conduct in the perils through which they had come had brought him at last to perceive that a woman may lack the simpering graces of cultured femininity, and yet because of that lack be the more admirable. He wondered what precisely might have been her earlier relations with Captain Blood, and was conscious of a certain uneasiness, which urged him now to probe the matter. His lordship's pale, dreamy eyes had, as I have said, a habit of observing things, and his wits were tolerably acute. He was blaming himself now for not having observed certain things before, or, at least, for not having studied them more closely, and he was busily connecting them with more recent observations made that very day.

He had observed, for instance, that Blood's ship was named the *Arabella,* and he knew that Arabella was Miss Bishop's name. And he had observed all the odd particulars of the meeting of Captain Blood and Miss Bishop, and the curious change that meeting had wrought in each.

The lady had been monstrously uncivil to the Captain. It was a very foolish attitude for a lady in her circumstances to adopt towards a man in Blood's; and his lordship could not imagine Miss Bishop as normally foolish. Yet, in spite of her rudeness, in spite of the fact that she was the niece of a man whom Blood must regard as his enemy, Miss Bishop and his lordship had been shown the utmost consideration aboard the Captain's ship. A cabin had been placed at the disposal of each, to which their scanty remaining belongings and Miss Bishop's woman had been duly transferred. They were given the freedom of the great cabin, and they had sat down to table with Pitt, the master, and Wolverstone, who was Blood's lieutenant, both of whom had shown them the utmost courtesy. Also there was the fact that Blood, himself, had kept almost studiously from intruding upon them.

His lordship's mind went swiftly but carefully down these avenues of thought, observing and connecting. Having exhausted them, he decided to seek additional information from Miss Bishop. For this he must wait until Pitt and Wolverstone should have withdrawn. He was hardly made to wait so long, for as Pitt rose from table to follow Wolverstone, who had already departed, Miss Bishop detained him with a question:

"Mr. Pitt," she asked, "were you not one of those who escaped from Barbados with Captain Blood?"

"I was. I, too, was one of your uncle's slaves."

"And you have been with Captain Blood ever since?"

"His shipmaster always, ma'am."

She nodded. She was very calm and self-contained; but his lordship observed that she was unusually pale, though considering what she had that day undergone this afforded no matter for wonder.

"Did you ever sail with a Frenchman named Cahusac?"

"Cahusac?" Pitt laughed. The name evoked a ridiculous memory. "Aye. He was with us at Maracaybo."

"And another Frenchman named Levasseur?"

His lordship marvelled at her memory of these names.

"Aye. Cahusac was Levasseur's lieutenant, until he died."

"Until who died?"

"Levasseur. He was killed on one of the Virgin Islands two years ago."

There was a pause. Then, in an even quieter voice than before, Miss Bishop asked:

"Who killed him?"

Pitt answered readily. There was no reason why he should not, though he began to find the catechism intriguing.

"Captain Blood killed him."

"Why?"

Pitt hesitated. It was not a tale for a maid's ears.

"They quarrelled," he said shortly.

"Was it about a . . . a lady?" Miss Bishop relentlessly pursued him.

"You might put it that way."

"What was the lady's name?"

Pitt's eyebrows went up; still he answered.

"Miss d'Ogeron. She was the daughter of the Governor of Tortuga. She had gone off with this fellow Levasseur, and . . . and Peter delivered her out of his dirty clutches. He was a black-hearted scoundrel, and deserved what Peter gave him."

"I see. And . . . and yet Captain Blood has not married her?"

"Not yet," laughed Pitt, who knew the utter groundlessness of the common gossip in Tortuga, which pronounced Mdlle. d'Ogeron the Captain's future wife.

Miss Bishop nodded in silence, and Jeremy Pitt turned to depart, relieved that the catechism was ended. He paused in the doorway to impart a piece of information.

"Maybe it'll comfort you to know that the Captain has altered our course for your benefit. It's his intention to put you both ashore on the coast of Jamaica, as near Port Royal as we dare venture. We've gone about, and if this wind holds ye'll soon be home again, mistress."

"Vastly obliging of him," drawled his lordship, seeing that Miss Bishop made no shift to answer. Sombre-eyed she sat, staring into vacancy.

"Indeed, ye may say so," Pitt agreed. "He's taking risks that few would take in his place. But that's always been his way."

He went out, leaving his lordship pensive, those dreamy blue eyes of his intently studying Miss Bishop's face for all their dreaminess; his mind increasingly uneasy. At length Miss Bishop looked at him, and spoke.

"Your Cahusac told you no more than the truth, it seems."

"I perceived that you were testing it," said his lordship. "I am wondering precisely why."

Receiving no answer, he continued to observe her silently, his long, tapering fingers toying with a ringlet of the golden periwig in which his long face was set.

Miss Bishop sat bemused, her brows knit, her brooding glance seeming to study the fine Spanish point that edged the tablecloth. At last his lordship broke the silence.

"He amazes me, this man," said he, in his slow, languid voice that never seemed to change its level. "That he should alter his course for us is in itself matter for wonder; but that he should take a risk on our behalf—that he should venture into Jamaica waters. . . . It amazes me, as I have said."

Miss Bishop raised her eyes, and looked at him. She appeared to be very thoughtful. Then her lip flickered curiously, almost scornfully, it seemed to him. Her slender fingers drummed the table.

"What is still more amazing is that he does not hold us to ransom," said she at last.

"It's what you deserve."

"Oh, and why, if you please?"

"For speaking to him as you did."

"I usually call things by their names."

"Do you? Stab me! I shouldn't boast of it. It argues either extreme youth or extreme foolishness." His lordship, you see, belonged to my Lord Sunderland's school of philosophy. He added after a moment: "So does the display of ingratitude."

A faint colour stirred in her cheeks. "Your lordship is evidently aggrieved with me. I am disconsolate. I hope your lordship's grievance is sounder than your views of life. It is news to me that ingratitude is a fault only to be found in the young and the foolish."

"I didn't say so, ma'am." There was a tartness in his tone evoked by the tartness she had used. "If you would do me the honour to listen, you would not misapprehend me. For if, unlike you, I do not always say precisely what I think, at least I say precisely what I wish to convey. To be ungrateful may be human; but to display it is childish."

"I ... I don't think I understand." Her brows were knit. "How have I been ungrateful and to whom?"

"To whom? To Captain Blood. Didn't he come to our rescue?"

"Did he?" Her manner was frigid. "I wasn't aware that he knew of our presence aboard the *Milagrosa*."

His lordship permitted himself the slightest gesture of impatience.

"You are probably aware that he delivered us," said he. "And living as you have done in these savage places of the world, you can hardly fail to be aware of what is known even in England: that this fellow Blood strictly confines himself to making war upon the Spaniards. So that to call him thief and pirate as you did was to overstate the case against him at a time when it would have been more prudent to have understated it."

"Prudence?" Her voice was scornful. "What have I to do with prudence?"

"Nothing—as I perceive. But, at least, study generosity. I tell you frankly, ma'am, that in Blood's place I should never have been so nice. Sink me! When you consider what he has suffered at the hands of his fellow-countrymen, you may marvel with me that he should trouble to discriminate between Spanish and English. To be sold into slavery! Ugh!" His lordship shuddered. "And to a damned colonial planter!" He checked abruptly. "I beg your pardon, Miss Bishop. For the moment . . ."

"You were carried away by your heat in defence of this . . . sea-robber." Miss Bishop's scorn was almost fierce.

His lordship stared at her again. Then he half-closed his large, pale eyes, and tilted his head a little. "I wonder why you hate him so," he said softly.

He saw the sudden scarlet flame upon her cheeks, the heavy frown that descended upon her brow. He had made her very angry, he judged. But there was no explosion. She recovered.

"Hate him? Lord! What a thought! I don't regard the fellow at all."

"Then ye should, ma'am." His lordship spoke his thought frankly. "He's worth regarding. He'd be an acquisition to the King's navy—a man that can do the things he did this morning. His service under de Ruyter wasn't wasted on him. That was a great seaman, and—blister me!—the pupil's worthy the master if I am a judge of anything. I doubt if the Royal Navy can show his equal. To thrust himself deliberately between those two, at point-blank range, and so turn the tables on them! It asks courage, resource, and invention. And we land-lubbers were not the only ones he tricked by his manoeuvre. That Spanish Admiral never guessed the intent until it was too late and Blood held him in check. A great man, Miss Bishop. A man worth regarding."

Miss Bishop was moved to sarcasm.

"You should use your influence with my Lord Sunderland to have the King offer him a commission."

His lordship laughed softly. "Faith, it's done already. I have his commission in my pocket." And he increased her amazement by a brief exposition of the circumstances. In that amazement he left her, and went in quest of Blood. But he was still intrigued. If she were a little less uncompromising in her attitude towards Blood, his lordship would have been happier.

He found the Captain pacing the quarterdeck, a man mentally exhausted from wrestling with the Devil, although of this particular occupation his lordship could have no possible suspicion. With the amiable familiarity he used, Lord Julian slipped an arm through one of the Captain's, and fell into step beside him.

"What's this?" snapped Blood, whose mood was fierce and raw. His lordship was not disturbed.

"I desire, sir, that we be friends," said he suavely.

"That's mighty condescending of you!"

Lord Julian ignored the obvious sarcasm.

"It's an odd coincidence that we should have been brought together in this fashion, considering that I came out to the Indies especially to seek you."

"Ye're not by any means the first to do that," the other scoffed. "But they've mainly been Spaniards, and they hadn't your luck."

"You misapprehend me completely," said Lord Julian. And on that he proceeded to explain himself and his mission.

When he had done, Captain Blood, who until that moment had stood still under the spell of his astonishment, disengaged his arm from his lordship's, and stood squarely before him.

"Ye're my guest aboard this ship," said he, "and I still have some notion of decent behaviour left me from other days, thief and pirate though I may be. So I'll not be telling you what I think of you for daring to bring me this offer, or of my Lord Sunderland—since he's your kinsman—for having the impudence to send it. But it does not surprise me at all that one who is a minister of James Stuart's should conceive that every man is to be seduced by bribes into betraying those who trust him." He flung out an arm in the direction of the waist, whence came the half-melancholy chant of the lounging buccaneers.

"Again you misapprehend me," cried Lord Julian, between concern and indignation. "That is not intended. Your followers will be included in your commission."

"And d'ye think they'll go with me to hunt their brethren—the Brethren of the Coast? On my soul, Lord Julian, it is yourself does the misapprehending. Are there not even notions of honour left in England? Oh, and there's more to it than that, even. D'ye think I could take a commission of King James's? I tell you I wouldn't be soiling my hands with it—thief and pirate's hands though they be. Thief and pirate is what you heard Miss Bishop call me to-day—a thing of scorn, an outcast. And who made me that? Who made me thief and pirate?"

"If you were a rebel . . ." his lordship was beginning.

"Ye must know that I was no such thing—no rebel at all. It wasn't even pretended. If it were, I could forgive them. But not even that cloak could they cast upon their foulness. Oh, no; there was no mistake. I was convicted for what I did, neither more nor less.

"That bloody vampire Jeffreys—bad cess to him!—sentenced me to death, and his worthy master James Stuart afterwards sent me into slavery, because I had performed an act of mercy; because compassionately and without thought for creed or politics I had sought to relieve the sufferings of a fellow-creature; because I had dressed the wounds of a man who was convicted of treason. That was all my offence. You'll find it in the records. And for that I was sold into slavery: because by the law of England, as administered by James Stuart in violation of the laws of God, who harbours or comforts a rebel is himself adjudged guilty of rebellion. D'ye dream, man, what it is to be a slave?"

He checked suddenly at the very height of his passion. A moment he paused, then cast it from him as if it had been a cloak. His voice sank again. He uttered a little laugh of weariness and contempt.

"But there! I grow hot for nothing at all. I explain myself, I think, and God knows, it is not my custom. I am grateful to you, Lord Julian, for your kindly intentions. I am so. But ye'll understand, perhaps. Ye look as if ye might."

Lord Julian stood still. He was deeply stricken by the other's words, the passionate, eloquent outburst that in a few sharp, clear-cut strokes had so convincingly presented the man's bitter case against humanity, his complete apologia and justification for all that could be laid to his charge. His lordship looked at that keen, intrepid face gleaming lividly in the light of the great poop lantern, and his own eyes were troubled. He was abashed.

He fetched a heavy sigh. "A pity," he said slowly. "Oh, blister me—a cursed pity!" He held out his hand, moved to it on a sudden generous impulse. "But no offence between us, Captain Blood!"

"Oh, no offence. But . . . I'm a thief and a pirate." He laughed without mirth, and, disregarding the proffered hand, swung on his heel.

Lord Julian stood a moment, watching the tall figure as it moved away towards the taffrail. Then, letting his arms fall helplessly to his sides in dejection, he departed.

Just within the doorway of the alley leading to the cabin, he ran into Miss Bishop. Yet she had not been coming out, for her back was towards him, and she was moving in the same direction. He followed her, his mind too full of Captain Blood to be concerned just then with her movements.

In the cabin he flung into a chair, and exploded with a violence altogether foreign to his nature.

"Damme if ever I met a man I liked better, or even a man I liked as well. Yet there's nothing to be done with him."

"So I heard," she admitted in a small voice. She was very white, and she kept her eyes upon her folded hands.

He looked up in surprise, and then sat conning her with brooding glance. "I wonder, now," he said presently, "if the mischief is of your working. Your words have rankled with him. He threw them at me again and again. He wouldn't take the King's commission; he wouldn't take my hand even. What's to be done with a fellow like that? He'll end on a yardarm for all his luck. And the quixotic fool is running into danger at the present moment on our behalf."

"How?" she asked him with a sudden startled interest.

"How? Have you forgotten that he's sailing to Jamaica, and that Jamaica is the headquarters of the English fleet? True, your uncle commands it . . ."

She leaned across the table to interrupt him, and he observed that her breathing had grown labored, that her eyes were dilating in alarm.

"But there is no hope for him in that!" she cried. "Oh, don't imagine it! He has no bitterer enemy in the world! My uncle is a

114

hard, unforgiving man. I believe that it was nothing but the hope of taking and hanging Captain Blood that made my uncle leave his Barbados plantations to accept the deputy-governorship of Jamaica. Captain Blood doesn't know that, of course . . . " She paused with a little gesture of helplessness.

"I can't think that it would make the least difference if he did," said his lordship gravely. "A man who can forgive such an enemy as Don Miguel and take up this uncompromising attitude with me isn't to be judged by ordinary rules. He's chivalrous to the point of idiocy."

"And yet he has been what he has been and done what he has done in these last three years," said she, but she said it sorrowfully now, without any of her earlier scorn.

Lord Julian was sententious, as I gather that he often was. "Life can be infernally complex," he sighed.

# A Lady among the Pirates

## *Fanny Loviot*

Towards four o'clock in the afternoon, on the 4th of October, 1854, I went on board the brig *Caldera*, which, under a Chilian flag, was about to set sail that evening for California. Such was the honesty and frankness of the captain's face that I was immediately prepossessed in his favour. Mr. Rooney was a man of about thirty-five years of age, neither short nor tall, and, to all appearance, a thorough sailor. His countenance betokened an energetic character, and I would have staked my existence upon his courage and good-nature. My first care was to visit my cabin, and arrange my luggage. Soon after this, we weighed anchor, and put out to sea. Once on the way, I was seized with a listless melancholy, for which I found it impossible to account. This melancholy, which might have been a presentiment, seemed all the stranger considering that I was returning to America, to my sister, and my friends. Resolved, somehow or another, to shake it off, I left my cabin and made the tour of the ship. It was a handsome three-masted brig of eight hundred tons burthen, well rigged, and gracefully built. I visited the saloon, the cabins, the captain's parlour, and another which belonged to the supercargo of a commercial house at San

Francisco, the heads of which had a valuable cargo on board. The saloon was lighted from above, and elegantly fitted up with panellings of white and gold. So clean and orderly was every corner of the vessel that it seemed as if nothing adverse could take place to interrupt our course; and I almost fancied that we might all be allowed to sleep away the three long months which must elapse before our arrival in California.

Of one of my fellow-travellers I shall often have occasion to speak. He was a Chinese of about fifty years of age, and an inhabitant of Canton. He had a commercial house at San Francisco, and was carrying with him a large stock of opium, sugar, and coffee. His name was Than-Sing. His features were of the type common to his nation, and deeply scarred by the small-pox. Though plain, however, he was not unprepossessing; for good-nature was expressed in every line of his countenance, and his smile was kindness itself.

We sat down four to dinner, and found that no two of us belonged to the same nation. The captain was English, the supercargo American, Than-Sing Chinese, and I French. I am thus particular in defining our several nationalities, in order to prove how much our difficulties must have been increased, in any case of peril, by the differences of language. Than-Sing spoke English as I did, that is to say, indifferently; but not one of the party spoke French. It will hereafter be seen how Than-Sing, who alone spoke Chinese, had it in his power to save and serve us all. Our crew consisted of seventeen men of various nations.

Awakened next morning by the hurrying to and fro of the sailors, I became uneasy, dressed in haste, and went on deck. A sailor had fallen overboard, and the ship was lying-to. His head was just visible above the waves, and we had already left him far behind. He followed us, swimming gallantly, and, in the course of about twenty minutes, came alongside, and was hoisted upon deck. His comrades greeted him with acclamations; but he replied roughly enough, as if he were ashamed of his misfortune.

Trifling as this incident was, it left an unpleasant impression on my mind, for it seemed as if our voyage had begun badly. The song of the sailors augmented my melancholy. It was a fantastic and monotonous melody, very unlike the cheerful airs sung by our French mariners. Going back sorrowfully to my cabin, I amused myself by feeding two charming little birds that I had brought with me from Hong-Kong. I kissed them tenderly: for they were all that I had to love.

The breeze was mild; we had land in sight all day, and made but little way. Towards evening the barometer fell with alarming rapidity, a strong wind sprang up, and the sea grew boisterous. Anticipating the coming storm, the captain made rapid preparations, and furled all sail. It was well he did so, for we were soon to be at the mercy of the typhoon. The typhoon is a dangerous wind, much feared in the Indian and Chinese seas. On the sea, as on the land, it carries with it death and destruction. It is neither a north wind nor a south wind, and blows as much from the east as from the west. It is, indeed, a combat between all four, and the great ocean is the scene of their warfare. Woe, then, to the ship which has to contend against this fearful strife! Tossed and tormented, driven on from behind, and driven back from before, neither sailors nor steersmen avail to guide her.

For long hours the *Caldera* remained the plaything of this fearful wind. We were every moment threatened with destruction. Before the tempest had lasted two hours the mizzen-mast and main-mast were both broken halfway, and the top-gallant masts laid along the decks, with all their cordage rent. Two of our boats had been carried away by the waves. Below, everything was broken, and we had two feet of water in the cabins. Added to all this, the waves broke against us with a noise like thunder, and our timbers creaked as if the ship would go to pieces.

Every now and then, the captain came down to console me. His hair and clothes were wet through; but, in the midst of all this danger, he never lost his cheerfulness for an instant. "You're afraid," said he, in his rough but kindly tones. I denied it; but my pale face betrayed my fears, for he shook his head compassionately as he left me.

I must confess that I endured an agony of terror. Everything was rolling about, and my poor little birds, hanging from the ceiling in their wicker cage, shrank down together, trembling and stupefied. For my part, I had taken refuge in my berth; for the motion was such, that I could no longer keep my footing. All at once a frightful crash resounded overhead, and I was flung out upon the floor. I covered my face with my hands—I believed that the ship was going to pieces, and that our last moments had arrived. This crash proved to be the fall of the mizzen and top-gallant masts. I marvel now that the *Caldera* should have lived through the storm. She did live, however, and after fourteen hours of distress, the tempest gradually abated. Towards midday, the wind died quite away, and, if the sea continued to be somewhat agitated, that agitation, after what we had lately gone through, seemed like a delightful calm.

About four o'clock in the afternoon, I left my cabin and went into the saloon. It was flooded with water, and strewn with a chaotic mass of broken furniture and crockery.

I then proceeded upon deck. There, indeed, the tempest had done its work. It was with difficulty that I could make my way from one end to the other. Cables, chains, and broken masts lay about in all directions. The sea was muddy, and the sky was low, and a thick haze hung over the distance. The sailors looked weary, and one of them had been severely wounded by a falling mast. Added to our other misfortunes, fifty-two fowls and six pigs had been killed during the night. We were still within sight of land, and the captain, whose object was to get back to Hong-Kong as soon as possible, had with difficulty hoisted a sail to the foremast. To return was imperative, since it would take at least six weeks to repair the damage that we had sustained. A dead calm now reigned around us, and we remembered for the first time that we were all very hungry. Our dinner was the dreariest meal imaginable. We were all profoundly silent. The captain's face betrayed his anxiety, and I afterwards learnt that he was thinking at that very time of a misfortune which happened to him only two years before. Falling into the hands of Indian pirates, Captain Rooney had seen all his sailors killed before his face, and, being himself bound to the mast of his ship, was cruelly tortured. For three months they kept him prisoner, at the end of which time he effected his escape.

So dismal a countenance as that of the supercargo I never beheld. He had been in mortal fear of death all through the night, and acknowledged that he had trembled almost as much for his cargo as for his life.

As for Than-Sing, his was the face of a man who openly rejoiced in his safety, and his calm smile contrasted strangely with the general uneasiness.

For my part, I could not so readily forget the sufferings of the last eighteen hours. "What more can I know of the horrors of the sea," I asked myself, "if it be not to make it my grave?"

The captain ordered us early to rest. I was so weary that I could have slept upon the floor as contentedly as upon a feather-bed, and my berth appeared to me the most delightful place in the world. I hoped to sleep for at least ten or twelve good hours, and had no sooner laid down than I fell into a profound slumber.

It might have been midnight, or perhaps a little later, when I awoke, believing myself to be the victim of a horrible night-mare. I seemed to hear a chorus of frightful cries, and, sitting up bewildered in my bed, found my cabin filled with a strange red light. Believing that the ship was on fire, I sprang out of bed and rushed to the door. The captain and the supercargo were stand-ing each on the threshold of his cabin. We looked speechlessly at one another, for the savage yells grew every instant louder, and a shower of missiles was falling all around. Pieces of stone and iron came crashing down through the skylights, and rolled heavily about the decks, and strange flashes of fire were reflected from without.

I clung to the captain—I could not speak—I had no voice, and the words died away upon my lips. "Captain!" I faltered; "Captain! fire!—the ship is on fire—do you hear?—what noise is that?" But he stood like one petrified. "I do not know," said he; and, rushing into his cabin, came back with a revolver in his hand. That revolver was the only weapon of defence on board. At this moment the mate came running down. I could not hear what he said but, dreading some terrible misfortune, I went back into my cabin and climbed up to the window that overlooked the sea. By the lurid light without, I beheld a crowd of Chinese junks. Beside myself with terror, I flew back to the captain, crying, "Oh, they are pirates! they are pirates!" And they were indeed pirates—those terrible pirates which scour the Chinese seas, and are so famous for their cruelties. We were utterly in their power. Three junks, each manned by thirty or forty ruffians, surrounded the *Caldera*. These creatures seemed like demons, born of the tempest, and bent upon completing our destruction. Having boarded the *Caldera* by means of grappling-hooks, they were now dancing an infernal dance upon deck, and uttering cries which sounded like nothing human. The smashing of the glass awoke our whole crew, and the light which we had taken for a fire at sea was occasioned by the bursting of fiery balls which they cast on deck to frighten us.

Calculating upon this method of alarming their victims, they attack vessels chiefly in the night, and seldom meet with any resistance. The captain, the supercargo, and the mate made an effort to go upon deck. I followed them instinctively. Driven back by flaming balls, we were forced to beat a retreat, and narrowly escaped being burnt. It seemed strange that they should risk setting fire to the ship, when plunder was their evident intention. The captain, having but his revolver for our defence, recommended that we should keep out of sight as long as possible. Useless precaution! Accustomed as they were to predatory warfare, they were sure to find us as easily in one place as another. Fear, however, left us no time for reflection. We fled precipitately between decks, and hid ourselves as best we might. Five of the sailors were there before us, and none of us knew what had become of the rest of the crew—perhaps they were already taken prisoners. As to Than-Sing, he had not been seen since the evening before.

These savage cries, and this still more savage dance, went on overhead without cessation. Through a crack in the partition which concealed us, we witnessed all their proceedings. Seen by the red firelight, they looked unspeakably hideous. They were dressed like all other Chinese, except that they wore scarlet turbans on their heads, and round their waists broad leathern belts garnished with knives and pistols. In addition to this, each man carried in his hand a naked sword. At this sight my heart sank within me, and I believed my last hour was at hand. Creeping on my hands and knees, I crouched down behind the captain, and we hid ourselves amid the merchandise, about twenty feet from the entrance. Further than this we could not go, on account of the goods which were there piled to the level of the upper deck. Scarcely able to breathe, we heard them come down into the cabins, and upset everything on which they could lay their hands. Soon a well-known voice reached our ears. It was the voice of Than-Sing, whom they had just discovered. A loud dispute then took place between him and the pirates. They doubtless demanded where the rest of the crew had hidden themselves;

for he called to us in English several times, saying, "Captain, captain! Where are you? Are you below? Answer! Come here! Come quickly!" But nobody stirred.

The captain grasped his pistol, and vowed to shoot the first pirate who came near us; but I entreated him to do no such thing, since the death of one man could in nowise serve us, and might, on the contrary, incline our enemies to a wholesale massacre. He seemed to see the justice of my fears, and hid his weapon in his bosom.

It was not long before we were discovered. I shudder still when I recall the sound of those approaching footsteps. They raised the trap on deck, and let down a lighted lantern. We crowded together in a vain effort at concealment; but the light came lower and lower, and we were seen at last. In another instant five or six pirates, armed to the teeth, leaped into the hold, and advanced towards us. The captain then rose up and went to meet them. Smiling, he offered them his revolver. They drew back, as if to defend themselves; then, seeing that he held the butt-end turned towards them, and that we made no effort at resistance, came eagerly forward, and glared at us with savage delight. Two of them then went up on deck, and made signs that we should follow them. More dead than alive, I remained crouched behind some bales. I saw my companions going, one by one. I would have followed them, but had no strength to stir. When the last had disappeared, and I found myself left alone with these monsters, I rose up by a despairing effort and fell at their feet. Seeing that I was a woman, they burst into exclamations of surprise and joy. Dreading every instant lest they should seize me, I rushed to the door, and in another moment found myself on deck.

Surrounded by a crowd of pirates armed with sabres and pistols, I saw every eye fixed eagerly upon the few jewels that I wore. To pull off my rings and ear-rings, and throw them at their feet, was the work of a moment, for I dreaded lest I should become the victim of their impatience. Those who were nearest clutched them greedily. An angry scuffle ensued, and but for the interference of their captain, a sanguinary quarrel would probably have followed. They then pushed me towards the stairs leading to the upper deck, and there I found my companions loaded with chains. The sea was still agitated, and huge black clouds, last remnants of the tempest, scudded hither and thither across the sky. The poor *Caldera*, riding helplessly at anchor, swayed to and fro like a mere log upon the waters. A thick fog froze us with cold, and a dead silence, which was only interrupted by the groans of the sailor who had been hurt the night before, reigned all around us. Torn by a thousand fears and regrets, I longed to weep, but could not shed a tear.

Meanwhile the pirates, who numbered, perhaps, a hundred men, were searching for plunder. Two or three of them came up, and made signs to me to observe the chains with which my companions were fettered. Thinking that they wished to treat me in the same manner, I submissively held out my hands, but they shook their heads. One of them then passed the cold blade of his sabre along my throat, whilst the others made signs expressive of their inclination to behead me. I stirred neither hand nor foot, though my face, I dare say, indicated the depth of my despair. Once more I extended my hands to be tied. They seized hold of them angrily, and passed their fingers round and round my wrists, though for what purpose I could not imagine. What could they want? Was it their intention to cut off my hands? In this moment I recognized all the horrors of my position. I closed my eyes, and leaned my head against the bulwark. The sight of these monsters was alone sufficient to make death welcome, and I awaited it with entire resignation. I was still in this state of semi-stupefaction when Than-Sing came up, and touched me on the shoulder. "Be not afraid," said he. "They do not mean to harm you. Their only object is to frighten you, lest you should attempt to set your companions at liberty."

He was now sent for by the pirate-chief, who was a small wiry-looking man with a countenance more intelligent and less ferocious than the others. Than-Sing, although not fettered, was a prisoner like ourselves, and, being the only Chinese on board, acted as our interpreter.

Captain Rooney was next sent for. Calm and disdainful, he seemed to despise the success of his captors and his own personal danger. "Is he English?" asked the chief. Than-Sing, luckily remembering the feud then existing between China and Great Britain, replied that the captain was a Spaniard, and the crew composed of various Europeans. This proved, indeed, to be a fortunate inspiration; for the pirate instantly replied that, had we been English, our throats should all have been cut upon the spot. He then enquired respecting the number of persons on board, and the amount of money which we carried, and ended by asking if I were the wife of Mr. Rooney. Having satisfied him on the two former points, Than-Sing replied that I was a French-woman, journeying to California, a stranger in China, and quite without friends or relatives in this part of the world. The excellent Chinese was careful to impress this fact of my loneliness upon them, hoping thereby to moderate any expectations which they might have formed respecting the amount of my ransom.

Captain Rooney's hands were then released, and he had to submit to the humiliation of accompanying the chief through every part of the ship. He was even obliged to furnish an exact inventory of his cargo. For our lives we were already indebted to the generous misrepresentations of Than-Sing; but it was yet possible that the pirates might change their minds, and although they had promised to save our lives, we scarcely dared to depend upon it. Besides all this, more pirates might arrive to dispute the prize, and we be sacrificed in the strife. Such were my reflections during the absence of the captain. A scene of plunder was at this moment being enacted before my eyes. The cabins were first dismantled; and I beheld my own luggage transported on board the junks. Everything was taken—even my dear little birds in their wicker cage. "They survived the tempest," said I, "only to die of cold and neglect!" And, with this, the tears which had so long refused to flow coursed hotly down my cheeks.

I was aroused from this melancholy train of thought by the return of the captain. Our sailors were now unchained to work the ship, and the pirate-chief gave orders that we should weigh anchor, and put into a neighbouring bay. At the same time our men were all given to understand that, at the least token of revolt, we should all be slaughtered without pity. As for Than-Sing, the supercargo, and myself, we were left on the upper deck in company with the wounded sailor, since none of us could be of use in the management of the vessel.

At this moment one of the robbers came up with a parcel of jewels and money, which he had just found. In one hand he held a silver fork, the properties and uses of which seemed mightily to perplex him. He paused, looked at me, and raised the fork to his head, as if to ask me whether it were a woman's comb. Under any other circumstances his ignorance might have amused me; now, however, I had no strength to reply to him even by a sign. Than-Sing then came to my assistance, and the pirate, having received the information he desired, went away. I hoped that we had got rid of him, but returning almost immediately, he held a handful of silver before my eyes, pointed towards a junk which we had in tow, and endeavoured, by his looks and gestures, to arouse me from my apathy. It was not difficult to interpret these signs, and I saw with a shudder that he wanted me to fly with him. Than-Sing, who had been silently observing this scene, now took pity on my distress, and addressed the man in Chinese. He doubtless threatened to betray his treachery to the chief; for the pirate hung his head, and went silently away.

The weather was now misty and much colder, and, half-clothed as we were, we suffered intensely. It is but fair, however, to say that our captors were not wholly insensible to our miseries, and that they had at least the charity to cover us with a few rugs and pieces of sail-cloth.

Shortly after this, we heard a sound of falling chains, and the anchor was cast once more. Alas! was that anchor ever to be weighed again, or was it destined to rust away throughout all the ages of time, in the spot where it was now imbedded? Heaven only knew!

Day broke, and the last shades of night faded and fled. The pirates assembled us on deck, counted us over to see that none were missing, lifted the hatches at the foot of the mainmast, and lowered us, one by one, into the hold. Some of them followed us down, and kept a savage watch upon our every movement. This last proceeding struck us with a mortal terror. Believing that our fate was just about to be decided, we sat down mournfully among the bales of goods, and waited like condemned criminals. Our jailers seemed now to be more cruelly disposed than ever. Every moment, and without any kind of provocation, they struck our poor sailors with the handles and flats of their sabres, and amused themselves by flourishing these weapons round my head and that of Captain Rooney. Presently they took to examining our wrists, and laughed to see the wounds which our chains had left upon them. Hearing a noise on deck, they, by and bye, left us; having first taken the precaution of battening down the hatches above our heads. Plunged into utter darkness, and almost suffocated for want of air, we endured this captivity for more than an hour. The hatches were then lifted, a flood of blinding sunlight poured in upon us, and the friendly voice of Than-Sing greeted us from above.

Up to the present time, as I have already shown, the Chinese merchant had had it in his power to render us important services. Of these he never wearied. He was our good genius. His presence alone inspired us with courage and endurance; and whenever he opened his mouth to interpose between our feebleness and the ferocity of his countrymen, our dangers seemed to diminish. His coolness never failed him for an instant. When he was not actually with us, pursuing his work of encouragement and comfort, he was negotiating in our favour. With that expression of calm serenity, his plain features became at times almost patriarchal; and I was amazed to find any Chinese gifted with qualities of such Christian charity.

During the hour which had just gone by, the question of life and death had probably been debated. Providence, however, had watched over us, and we were once more spared. It was now decided by the pirate-chief that our crew should be set to work to unlade the vessel.

The valuable freight of opium which we had on board was the property of Than-Sing, who was accordingly sent below with Captain Rooney to assist the pirates in clearing out these stores. The sailors then passed the packages from hand to hand; the pirates formed a chain from junk to junk; and the bales of sugar, rice, coffee, and other goods were speedily transferred.

Forgotten in the midst of this excitement, I sat alone and watched the work of spoilation.

After about an hour's labour, our sailors were allowed to rest for a few moments, and received a scanty ration of biscuits and water. Several of the poor fellows offered me a share of their food; but, although I eagerly drank what water they could spare me, I found it impossible to eat a morsel. For long hours my throat and chest had been on fire, and I suffered cruelly from thirst.

Soon after this, Than-Sing and the captain came in search of me. Thankful was I, indeed, to see them, for the pirates had of late been thronging around me with gesticulations which filled me with uneasiness. My friends then led me to a cabin at the other end of the vessel, where I hoped to be left without molestation. Crossing the deck, I saw that we had anchored close in shore, and were surrounded by an immense amphitheatre of wooded hills. At any other time I should have been charmed with this exquisite scene; but the sight of the *Caldera*, now a mere wreck, usurped all my attention. Her broken masts were lying along deck—fragments of doors and windows lay scattered all about—the compass had been carried away, and the helm was broken. Add to this the ferocious cries of our barbarian captors, and the picture is complete. I was glad to hurry away from this sight; but our pretty cabins were no longer recognizable.

Lying upon a large green velvet sofa, which was the only article of furniture left entire, I yielded to an access of the profoundest melancholy. Every moment the pirates kept passing to and fro, or coming in to cast lots for such of the booty as was yet unshared amongst them. Remembering how they had refused to tie my hands, and the little likelihood I had for supposing them to be actuated by any feeling of compassion or respect, I recalled some frightful stories read in times gone by, and dreaded lest I should become the victim of their brutality. Sooner than this, I resolved to throw myself into the sea. That I should now be living to write these lines—that I should now be relating the long story of my sufferings—seems, if I may dare to say so, like a special manifestation of that divine goodness which measures the trial by the strength of the sufferer.

Our provisions, with the exception of some rice and a few biscuits, had all been carried on board the three junks. Our sailors had been allowed no rest. Groaning under fatigues, which were enforced with the sword, they laboured on till night-fall, and even then, but for the intercessions of Than-Sing, would have been allowed no sleep.

My companions slept in the cabin adjoining mine, and we were allowed to close our doors for the night. Having eaten nothing all day, and being kept awake, moreover, by the vociferations of the pirates, whose numbers had lately been increased by the arrival of fresh junks, I passed a miserable night. Many a time, during these long hours of wakefulness, I opened my little window and leaned out into the air; but each time that I did so, my terrors were increased by the sight of these demons quarrelling over their booty. Day dawned, and a sudden rumour spread all at once throughout the ship. Starting from their sleep, our sailors rushed on deck, and two or three came down crying, "The pirates are leaving us! The pirates are leaving us!" A wild and sudden hope possessed us. We believed that help was at hand, and that the moment of our release had arrived. Could it be the approach of a steamer which caused the flight of our captors? A single glance, however, was sufficient. Alas! that which we had supposed to be a deliverance proved to be but an added danger. Our pirates were indeed leaving us, but a new flotilla was bearing down upon us with all sail set! For more than a quarter of an hour we were left alone in the wreck, and Than-Sing explained to us that the small junks were making off with their booty, for fear it should be wrested from them by the new comers. These second enemies were, then, fiercer and more numerous than the first! What would they do with us? What would now become of us? What had we to expect? We counted the minutes as they passed, and the junks drew rapidly nearer.

I felt my very heart sink within me, and all the horrors to which I might be subjected rushed across my mind. "Oh, captain," said I, "I shall die with fear! Can you not help to disguise me? Let me be dressed as you are! What shall I do? I am a woman, and these monsters are coming! Have pity on me! Have pity on me!" "Yes, you are right," said Captain Rooney, kindly and compassionately. Having on two pairs of trousers, he then gave me one. We next found a shirt and a Chinese jacket, and one of the sailors gave me his cap, beneath which I gathered up my hair. I had but one hair-pin left, and on my naked feet a pair of slippers. Hastening into my cabin, I dressed rapidly, and had scarcely completed this transformation when loud shouts proclaimed the approach of our new enemies. The small junks, which had fled before the others like startled water-fowl, were already far away. We hid ourselves in one of the after-cabins, and the captain grouped his men in such a manner as might best conceal me. He and Than-Sing stood before me, and in another moment the pirates were on board. About forty junks now surrounded the *Caldera,* each junk carrying from twenty to forty men, and the large ones being mostly mounted with ten or twelve cannons.

The pirates of the Chinese seas make their junks their homes, and carry their wives and children with them on every expedition.

The women assist in working the ships, and are chiefly employed in lading and unlading the merchandise. As for the children, they carry them upon their backs in a kind of bag till they are able to run alone. Each junk is commanded by a chief, and such is the terror of the pirate-name that, in a country which numbers three hundred and sixty millions of inhabitants, they ravage the seas with impunity. It sometimes happens that they have feuds among themselves, and many a piratical sea-fight takes place, in which the victory rests with the strongest.

Hidden as we were in a lower cabin, we heard these barbarians rush upon our decks with the force of a torrent that had burst its flood-gates. The first junks having carried away but a small portion of our cargo, these new pirates found an ample prize remaining. They therefore employed themselves in pillaging the ship, without taking the trouble to seek for us. Presently, such of the junks as were sufficiently laden dropped away, and set sail for those villages along the coast where they were in the habit of taking refuge. In the meantime, despite the indifference with which they treated us, fresh fears assailed us. We dreaded lest they should exhaust our store of provisions, and found ere long that these apprehensions were but too well grounded. Soon, a sack of rice, and a small bag of biscuits alone remained, and even these they would have taken from us, but for our urgent supplications.

We were now utterly destitute. For two days and more, we could scarcely be said to have eaten anything, and, faint with exhaustion, we abandoned ourselves to despair. As if animated with the very spirit of destruction, the pirates demolished everything which came in their way. The panellings in the saloon, the looking-glasses, the windows, the doors, and such of the furniture as was not already destroyed, they smashed into a thousand pieces. They carried away the very hinges and fastenings from off the doors, and even the green velvet divan, which had hitherto been left on account of its size. The deck was strewn all over with tea, coffee, sugar, biscuit, fragments of broken glass, and merchandise.

We were constantly obliged to turn out our pockets, in proof that we kept nothing back; and these monsters pressed around us, every now and then, in such numbers that we could scarcely move or breathe. My dress, which I had hidden as best I could, was found and carried off like everything else; and Than-Sing, who had chanced to take off his slippers for a moment, saw them snatched up and appropriated in the twinkling of an eye. The poor man was more annoyed by this loss than by all his previous misfortunes, for the slippers were made after the fashion of his country. Hereafter, one of our sailors, who was indifferently skilful in such matters, contrived to make him a new pair out of some fragments of leather which he found about the deck.

Cast upon the mercy of these savages, our situation was inexpressibly horrible. They were not deceived by my costume, for they surrounded me with eager curiosity, and asked Than-Sing if I were the wife of the captain. These questions filled me with terror, and I entreated Mr. Rooney to let me pass for his wife. They gathered round us in brutal mockery, asking if we wished to go to Hong-Kong; and then, finding that we were silent, laughed in our faces. Some of them, who seemed more savage and cruel than the rest, seized our sailors by the hair and flourished their sabres threateningly before their eyes; whilst I, sinking, and sick at heart, shrank down in a corner and hoped to be forgotten. Slender indeed was the tenure upon which we now held our lives! Who knows what might have happened had one single drop of blood been actually shed?

That same day, one of these men came when none of the rest were by, and talked for some time with Than-Sing. I saw the merchant's face light up as the conversation progressed, and the breathless eagerness with which he replied. The pirate was offering, as I afterwards learnt, to effect our escape; and Captain Rooney, by help of Than-Sing, agreed on the amount of our ransom. We were to be landed at Hong-Kong, and, meanwhile, were desired to hold ourselves in readiness for the first chance of escape. Two others came shortly after upon the same errand but, whether the reward which we offered was insufficient to recompense them for the danger or whether they dreaded the discovery of their treason, I know not—at all events, not one of the three kept his word, and we saw them no more.

Towards the evening of this day our sailors complained bitterly of hunger. We feared being left to all the agonies of starvation; but, in the midst of our distress, help came whence we had least reason to expect it. Amongst these robbers there was one who seemed actuated by sentiments of compassion. He came to us every now and then, appeared to sympathize with our distress, and, by and bye, pointed out his wife and children on board a neighbouring junk. Pleased to observe the interest with which we looked upon his family, this pirate, at the very moment when we were deploring our hunger, came back with a dish of rice and a huge bowl filled with some kind of Chinese ragoût, dressed after the Chinese fashion with a thick saffron-coloured sauce. Our poor fellows, little used to dainties, devoured it eagerly. But I could only just touch it with my lips, for the odour of it disgusted me. I contrived, however, to alleviate my hunger with a few spoonfuls of the rice. Towards night, the junks let go the grappling-irons, and put out to sea. It seemed scarcely probable that they would return again in equal numbers, since our plundered state must soon become known throughout the pirate-villages which line that coast.

Their departure left us at least the prospect of a quiet night; but, on the other hand, our ship was dismantled, and we had no available means of action. Had our enemies indeed abandoned us to die slowly of hunger, exposed to all the burning heat of a tropical sun, and swayed helplessly to and fro upon the great ocean, thousands of leagues from our homes and families? Than-Sing had ascertained that we were about twenty miles from Macao. Far away, he said, between two mountains which were just visible on the horizon, lay the city. This knowledge only served to make us still more miserable. Life was there, safety was there, and yet we could do nothing to help ourselves! If even we had succeeded in weighing the anchor, what chance had we, in our dismasted state, of drifting into any place of shelter? Glad to forget our anxieties, if but for a few hours, we all lay down to sleep.

What a picture it was! We had constructed a kind of rude oil-lamp, which cast a flickering glare around the cabin. This room, once so cheerful and pretty, now more nearly resembled some hideous dungeon. Seeing these rough sailors stretched about the floor, these upturned faces weary with suffering, these dismantled walls, and this air of general desolation, I began almost to tremble for my reason. Being so wretched, what more had I to fear? What were death to one whose sufferings had already touched the bounds of human endurance? One by one my companions sank away to sleep, and I alone remained, wakeful and sorrowful, to meditate the chances of our destiny. I questioned my past life; I searched all the corners of my memory; I asked myself what I had done to merit this great trial? Gladly would I have discovered any fault deserving such retribution, for I could not endure to doubt the justice of Heaven.

It might now have been about ten o'clock at night. I had tried in vain to sleep, and could not keep my eyes closed for five minutes together. Torn by a thousand different emotions, I lay and listened to the silence, till, carried away by an irresistible excitement, I rose, made my way on deck, and, flinging myself wearily down, gazed up at the sky and the stars. The moon shone like a silver mirror and, seeing the stillness and solitude of the night, I could not help fancying that something might yet be done towards our deliverance. Going back into the cabin, I roused Captain Rooney, and entreated him to come with me on deck. Somewhat surprised at this request, he rose and followed me. No sooner had we gone up, than we heard a sound of voices close under our lee, and found that a small junk was still lying alongside of us. The captain eagerly bent forward, as if to count the number of our enemies. They could not have been more than eight or ten. Having attentively observed them, he became profoundly silent. Amazed at his apathy, I dragged him towards the jolly-boat, which was yet hanging amid-ships, and said, "Well, captain, why do you not rouse your men?" He looked at me with a kind of weary wonder, as if scarcely able to comprehend my meaning. "Will you then do nothing?" said I. "Are you content patiently to await all the horrors of the future? Woman as I am, I would prefer a thousand times to dare something for my safety than linger here to die by violence or starvation! We are but twenty miles from Macao. This boat will hold us all. Once at sea, it is scarcely likely that the pirates, busy as they are, will observe our flight. Should they even see us, they might no longer care to follow us. Captain, in the name of all that is dear to you, let us at least make the attempt!"

Captain Rooney paused, remained for a few moments lost in thought, and then went quickly back into the cabin. "Rouse up!" said he, "rouse up, all of you! How can you sleep while we are yet in so much danger?" Laying aside his old habits of command, he then consulted them respecting our common danger, and suggested a plan of escape. At the first word of this proposition, the sailors turned disobediently away. "You do not deserve the name of men," said the captain, angrily. "I blush to think that a woman should be braver than you! She has the courage to prefer death to delay, and while flight yet offers us some chance of safety, you hesitate, you tremble, you behave like cowards! I see fear in every eye! No, I repeat it—no, you have not even the courage of a woman!"

Captain Rooney's plan was this: He proposed that his crew should steal softly upon deck, take the junk by surprise, and slay the eight Chinese by whom it was manned. We might then, without loss of time, set sail for Macao, where we should, in all probability, arrive before daybreak.

I remained silent whilst this consultation was going forward. My wisest course was to remain passive, in order that these men should not have it in their power to say that I proposed such bloodshed. That they did so accuse me was sufficiently plain, and yet I protest that in this suggestion I had no share whatever. The captain had not confided his projects to me; he had simply relied on my courage and co-operation, and had held me up to the men as an example for the mere sake of putting them to shame.

"Captain," said the supercargo, glancing angrily towards me, "that woman is mad; and, if it be by her advice that you are acting, we but consult the dictates of reason in refusing to obey you. This attempt could end only in destruction. Granting that we succeeded in capturing the junk, we should assuredly be overtaken, in the night, by others of the pirates, and they, guessing the means by which we had obtained possession of their cursed junk, would slay us all, without mercy."

There was justice in what he said, and the captain then fell back upon the plan which I had first proposed. It was agreed that the boat should be emptied of the coals with which it was now half-filled, and lowered into the water. While the men were busy at this work, I wandered to and fro about the deck and, searching amidst the debris, found some fragments of my dear home-letters. They were all torn and soiled, and I gathered them together with a sigh. At this moment, as if for the very purpose of favouring our flight, the last junk put off, and hove away to sea, leaving us alone for the first time since our captivity. Being now enabled to work with less precaution, the men redoubled their efforts, and the boat was soon unloaded. Eagerly and anxiously we crowded round, and examined it. Alas, how great was our disappointment! Several planks had started in the bottom of the boat, and she was no longer sea-worthy. Intense as was their discouragement, our sailors persisted in the attempt. A dull splash followed. We hung over the side of the vessel, and breathlessly prayed to Heaven for help and protection.

Ten minutes thus passed by. "It cannot be done," said the captain, falteringly; "she is already half-full of water." We looked into each others' faces, and silently dispersed. Great sorrows are dumb. Till to-morrow nothing could now be done, and who could tell what that morrow might bring forth?

# Pieces of Eight

### *Robert Louis Stevenson*

"I'll tell you what I've heard myself," continued Captain Smollett; "that you have a map of an island; that there's crosses on the map to show where treasure is; and that the island lies—" And then he named the latitude and longitude exactly.

"I never told that," cried the squire, "to a soul."

"The hands know it, sir," returned the captain.

"Livesey, that must have been you or Hawkins," cried the squire.

"It doesn't much matter who it was," replied the doctor. And I could see that neither he nor the captain paid much regard to Mr. Trelawney's protestations. Neither did I, to be sure, he was so loose a talker; yet in this case I believe he was really right, and that nobody had told the situation of the island.

"Well, gentlemen," continued the captain, "I don't know who has this map, but I make it a point it shall be kept secret even from me and Mr. Arrow. Otherwise I would ask you to let me resign."

"I see," said the doctor. "You wish us to keep this matter dark, and to make a garrison of the stern part of the ship, manned with my friend's own people, and provided with all the arms and powder on board. In other words, you fear a mutiny."

"Sir," said Captain Smollett, "with no intention to take offense, I deny your right to put words into my mouth. No captain, sir, would be justified in going to sea at all if he had ground enough to say that. As for Mr. Arrow, I believe him thoroughly honest; some of the men are the same; all may be for what I know. But I am responsible for the ship's safety and the life of every man Jack aboard of her. I see things going, as I think, not quite right; and I ask you to take certain precautions, or let me resign my berth. And that's all."

"Captain Smollett," began the doctor, with a smile, "did ever you hear the fable of the mountain and the mouse? You'll excuse me, I dare say, but you remind me of that fable. When you came in here I'll stake my wig you meant more than this."

"Doctor," said the captain, "you are smart. When I came in here I meant to get discharged. I had no thought that Mr. Trelawney would hear a word."

"No more I would," cried the squire. "Had Livesey not been here I should have seen you to the deuce. As it is, I have heard you. I will do as you desire, but I think the worse of you."

"That's as you please, sir," said the captain. "You'll find I do my duty."

And with that he took his leave.

"Trelawney," said the doctor, "contrary to all my notions, I believe you have managed to get two honest men on board with you—that man and John Silver."

"Silver, if you like," cried the squire, "but as for that intolerable humbug, I declare I think his conduct unmanly, unsailorly, and downright un-English."

"Well," said the doctor, "we shall see."

When we came on deck the men had begun already to take out the arms and powder, *yo-ho*-ing at their work, while the captain and Mr. Arrow stood by superintending.

The new arrangement was quite to my liking. The whole schooner had been overhauled; six berths had been made astern, out of what had been the after-part of the main hold, and this set of cabins was only joined to the galley and forecastle by a sparred passage on the port side. It had been originally meant that the captain, Mr. Arrow, Hunter, Joyce, the doctor, and the squire were to occupy these six berths. Now Redruth and I were to get two of them, and Mr. Arrow and the captain were to sleep on deck in the companion, which had been enlarged on each side till you might almost have called it a round-house. Very low it was still, of course, but there was room to swing two hammocks, and even the mate seemed pleased with the arrangement. Even he, perhaps, had been doubtful as to the crew, but that is only a guess, for, as you shall hear, we had not long the benefit of his opinion.

We were all hard at work changing the powder and the berths, when the last man or two, and Long John along with them, came off in a shore-boat.

The cook came up the side like a monkey for cleverness, and, as soon as he saw what was doing, "So ho, mates!" said he, "what's this!"

"We're a-changing the powder, Jack," answers one.

"Why, by the powers," cried Long John, "if we do, we'll miss the morning tide!"

"My orders!" said the captain, shortly. "You may go below, my man. Hands will want supper."

"Ay, ay, sir," answered the cook; and, touching his forelock, he disappeared at once in the direction of his galley.

"That's a good man, captain," said the doctor.

"Very likely, sir," replied Captain Smollett. "Easy with that, men—easy," he ran on, to the fellows who were shifting the powder; and then suddenly observing me examining the swivel we carried amidships, a long brass nine—"Here, you ship's boy," he cried, "out o' that! Off with you to the cook and get some work."

And then as I was hurrying off I heard him say, quite loudly, to the doctor:

"I'll have no favorites on my ship."

I assure you I was quite of the squire's way of thinking, and hated the captain deeply.

All that night we were in a great bustle getting things stowed in their place, and boatfuls of the squire's friends, Mr. Blandly and the like, coming off to wish him a good voyage and a safe return. We never had a night at the "Admiral Benbow" when I had half the work; and I was dog-tired when, a little before dawn, the boatswain sounded his pipe, and the crew began to man the capstan bars. I might have been twice as weary, yet I would not have left the deck, all was so new and interesting to me—the brief commands, the shrill notes of the whistle, the men bustling to their places in the glimmer of the ship's lanterns.

"Now, Barbecue, tip us a stave," cried one voice.

"The old one," cried another.

"Ay, ay, mates," said Long John, who was standing by, with his crutch under his arm, and at once broke out in the air and words I knew so well:

*"Fifteen men on the dead man's chest"*

And then the whole crew bore chorus:

*"Yo-ho-ho and a bottle of rum!"*

And at the third "ho!" drove the bars before them with a will.

Even at that exciting moment it carried me back to the old "Admiral Benbow" in a second, and I seemed to hear the voice of the captain piping in the chorus. But soon the anchor was short up; soon it was hanging dripping at the bows; soon the sails began to draw, and the land and shipping to flit by on either side, and before I could lie down to snatch an hour of slumber the *Hispaniola* had begun her voyage to the Isle of Treasure.

I am not going to relate the voyage in detail. It was fairly prosperous. The ship proved to be a good ship, the crew were capable seamen, and the captain thoroughly understood his business. But before we came the length of Treasure Island, two or three things had happened which require to be known.

Mr. Arrow, first of all, turned out even worse than the captain had feared. He had no command among the men, and people did what they pleased with him. But that was by no means the worst of it; for after a day or two at sea he began to appear on deck with hazy eye, red cheeks, tuttering tongue, and other marks of drunkenness. Time after time he was ordered below in disgrace. Sometimes he fell and cut himself; sometimes he lay all day long in his little bunk at one side of the companion;

sometimes for a day or two he would be almost sober and attend to his work at least passably.

In the meantime we could never make out where he got the drink. That was the ship's mystery. Watch him as we pleased, we could do nothing to solve it, and when we asked him to his face, he would only laugh, if he were drunk, and if he were sober, deny solemnly that he ever tasted anything but water.

He was not only useless as an officer, and a bad influence among the men, but it was plain that at this rate he must soon kill himself outright, so nobody was much surprised, nor very sorry, when one dark night, with a head sea, he disappeared entirely and was seen no more.

"Overboard!" said the captain. "Well, gentlemen, that saves the trouble of putting him in irons."

But there we were, without a mate, and it was necessary, of course, to advance one of the men. The boatswain, Job Anderson, was the likeliest man aboard, and though he kept his old title, he served in a way as mate. Mr. Trelawney had followed the sea, and his knowledge made him very useful, for he often took a watch himself in easy weather. And the coxswain, Israel Hands, was a careful, wily, old, experienced seaman who could be trusted at a pinch with almost anything.

He was a great confidant of Long John Silver, and so the mention of his name leads me on to speak of our ship's cook, Barbecue, as the men called him.

Aboard ship he carried his crutch by a lanyard round his neck, to have both hands as free as possible. It was something to see him wedge the foot of the crutch against a bulkhead, and, propped against it, yielding to every movement of the ship, get on with his cooking like someone safe ashore. Still more strange was it to see him in the heaviest of weather cross the deck. He had a line or two rigged up to help him across the widest spaces—Long John's earrings, they were called—and he would hand himself from one place to another, now using the crutch, now trailing it alongside by the lanyard, as quickly as another man could walk. Yet some of the men who had sailed with him before expressed their pity to see him so reduced.

"He's no common man, Barbecue," said the coxswain to me. "He had good schooling in his young days, and can speak like a book when so minded; and brave—a lion's nothing alongside of Long John! I seen him grapple four and knock their heads together—him unarmed."

All the crew respected and even obeyed him. He had a way of talking to each, and doing everybody some particular service. To me he was unweariedly kind, and always glad to see me in the galley, which he kept as clean as a new pin; the dishes hanging up burnished, and his parrot in a cage in the corner.

"Come away, Hawkins," he would say; "come and have a yarn with John. Nobody more welcome than yourself, my son. Sit you down and hear the news. Here's Cap'n Flint—I calls my parrot Cap'n Flint, after the famous buccaneer—here's Cap'n Flint predicting success to our v'yage. Wasn't you, Cap'n?"

And the parrot would say, with great rapidity: "Pieces of eight! Pieces of eight! Pieces of eight!" till you wondered that it was not out of breath or till John threw his handkerchief over the cage.

"Now, that bird," he would say, "is, may be, two hundred years old, Hawkins—they live forever mostly, and if anybody's seen more wickedness it must be the devil himself. She's sailed with England—the great Cap'n England, the pirate. She's been at Madagascar, and at Malabar, and Surinam, and Providence, and Portobello. She was at the fishing up of the wrecked plate ships. It's there she learned 'Pieces of eight,' and little wonder; three hundred and fifty thousand of 'em, Hawkins! She was at the boarding of the Viceroy of the Indies out of Goa, she was, and to look at her you would think she was a babby. But you smelt powder—didn't you, cap'n?"

"Stand by to go about," the parrot would scream.

"Ah, she's a handsome craft, she is," the cook would say, and give her sugar from his pocket, and then the bird would peck at the bars and swear straight on, passing belief for wickedness. "There," John would add, "you can't touch pitch and not be mucked, lad. Here's this poor old innocent bird of mine swearing blue fire and none the wiser, you may lay to that. She would swear the same, in a manner of speaking, before the chaplain." And John would touch his forelock with a solemn way he had, that made me think he was the best of men.

In the meantime the squire and Captain Smollett were still on pretty distant terms with one another. The squire made no bones about the matter; he despised the captain. The captain, on his part, never spoke but when he was spoken to, and then sharp and short and dry, and not a word wasted. He owned, when driven into a corner, that he seemed to have been wrong about the crew; that some of them were as brisk as he wanted to see, and all had behaved fairly well. As for the ship, he had taken a downright fancy to her. "She'll lie a point nearer the wind than a man has a right to expect of his own married wife, sir. But," he would add, "all I say is, we're not home again, and I don't like the cruise."

The squire, at this, would turn away and march up and down the deck, chin in air.

"A trifle more of that man," he would say, "and I should explode."

We had some heavy weather, which only proved the qualities of the *Hispaniola*. Every man on board seemed well content, and they must have been hard to please if they had been otherwise, for it is my belief there was never a ship's company so spoiled since Noah put to sea. Double grog was going on the least excuse; there was duff on odd days, as, for instance, if the squire heard it was any man's birthday; and always a barrel of apples standing broached in the waist, for anyone to help himself that had a fancy.

"Never knew good to come of it yet," the captain said to Doctor Livesey. "Spoil foc's'le hands, make devils. That's my belief."

But good did come of the apple barrel, as you shall hear, for if it had not been for that we should have had no note of warning and might all have perished by the hand of treachery.

This is how it came about.

We had run up the trades to get the wind of the island we were after—I am not allowed to be more plain—and now we were running down for it with a bright lookout day and night. It was about the last day of our outward voyage, by the largest computation; some time that night, or, at latest, before noon of the morrow, we should sight the Treasure Island. We were heading south-southwest, and had a steady breeze abeam and a quiet sea. The *Hispaniola* rolled steadily, dipping her bowsprit now and then with a whiff of spray. All was drawing alow and aloft; everyone was in the bravest spirits, because we were now so near an end of the first part of our adventure.

Now, just after sundown, when all my work was over and I was on my way to my berth, it occurred to me that I should like an apple. I ran on deck. The watch was all forward looking out for the island. The man at the helm was watching the luff of the sail and whistling away gently to himself, and that was the only sound excepting the swish of the sea against the bows and around the sides of the ship.

In I got bodily into the apple barrel, and found there was scarce an apple left; but, sitting down there in the dark, what with the sound of the waters and the rocking movement of the ship, I had either fallen asleep, or was on the point of doing so, when a heavy man sat down with rather a clash close by. The barrel shook as he leaned his shoulders against it, and I was just about to jump up when the man began to speak. It was Silver's voice, and, before I had heard a dozen words, I would not have shown myself for all the world, but lay there, trembling and listening, in the extreme of fear and curiosity; for from these dozen words I understood that the lives of all the honest men aboard depended upon me alone.

"No, not I," said Silver. "Flint was cap'n; I was quartermaster, along of my timber leg. The same broadside I lost my leg, old

Pew lost his deadlights. It was a master surgeon, him that ampy-tated me—out of college and all—Latin by the bucket, and what not; but he was hanged like a dog, and sun-dried like the rest, at Corso Castle. That was Roberts' men, that was, and comed of changing names to their ships—*Royal Fortune* and so on. Now, what a ship was christened, so let her stay, I says. So it was with the *Cassandra,* as brought us all safe home from Malabar, after England took the *Viceroy of the Indies;* so it was with the old *Walrus,* Flint's old ship, as I've seen a-muck with the red blood and fit to sink with gold."

"Ah!" cried another voice, that of the youngest hand on board, and evidently full of admiration, "he was the flower of the flock, was Flint!"

"Davis was a man, too, by all accounts," said Silver. "I never sailed along of him; first with England, then with Flint, that's my story; and now here on my own account, in a manner of speaking. I laid by nine hundred safe, from England, and two thousand after Flint. That ain't bad for a man before the mast—all safe in bank. Tain't earning now, it's saving does it, you may lay to that. Where's all England's men now? I dunno. Where's Flint's? Why, most of 'em aboard here, and glad to get the duff—been begging before that, some of 'em. Old Pew, as had lost his sight, and might have thought shame, spends twelve hundred pounds in a year, like a lord in Parliament. Where is he now? Well, he's dead now and under hatches; but for two years before that, shiver my timbers! The man was starving. He begged, and he stole, and he cut throats, and starved at that, by the powers!"

"Well, it ain't much use, after all," said the young seaman.

"'Tain't much use for fools, you may lay to it—that, nor noth-ing," cried Silver. "But now, you look here; you're young, you are, but you're as smart as paint. I see that when I set my eyes on you, and I'll talk to you like a man."

You can imagine how I felt when I heard this abominable old rogue addressing another in the very same words of flattery as he had used to myself. I think, if I had been able, that I would have killed him through the barrel. Meantime he ran on, little supposing he was overheard.

"Here it is about gentlemen of fortune. They lives rough, and they risk swinging, but they eat and drink like fighting-cocks, and when a cruise is done, why it's hundreds of pounds instead of hundreds of farthings in their pockets. Now, the most goes for rum and a good fling, and to sea again in their shirts. But that's not the course I lay. I puts it all away, some here, some there, and none too much anywheres, by reason of suspicion. I'm fifty, mark you; once back from this cruise I set up gentleman in earnest. Time enough, too, says you. Ah, but I've lived easy in the meantime; never denied myself o' nothing heart desires, and slept soft and ate dainty all my days, but when at sea. And how did I begin? Before the mast, like you!"

"Well," said the other, "but all the other money's gone now, ain't it? You daren't show face in Bristol after this."

"Why, where might you suppose it was?" asked Silver, derisively.

"At Bristol, in banks and places," answered his companion.

"It were," said the cook; "it were when we weighed anchor. But my old missis has it all by now. And the *Spy-glass* is sold, lease and good will and rigging; and the old girl's off to meet me. I would tell you where, for I trust you; but it 'ud make jealousy among the mates."

"And you can trust your missis?" asked the other.

"Gentlemen of fortune," returned the cook, "usually trust little among themselves, and right they are, you may lay to it. But I have a way with me, I have. When a mate brings a slip on his cable—one as knows me, I mean—it won't be in the same world with old John. There was some that was feared of Pew, and some that was feared of Flint; but Flint his own self was feared of me. Feared he was, and proud. They was the roughest crew afloat, was Flint's; the devil himself would have been feared to go to sea with them. Well, now, I tell you, I'm not a boasting man, and you seen yourself how easy I keep company; but when I was quartermaster, lambs wasn't the word for Flint's old buccaneers. Ah, you may be sure of yourself in old John's ship."

"Well, I tell you now," replied the lad, "I didn't half a quarter like the job till I had this talk with you, John, but there's my hand on it now."

"And a brave lad you were, and smart, too," answered Silver, shaking hands so heartily that all the barrel shook, "and a finer figurehead for a gentleman of fortune I never clapped my eyes on."

By this time I had begun to understand the meaning of their terms. By a "gentleman of fortune" they plainly meant neither more nor less than a common pirate, and the little scene that I had overheard was the last act in the corruption of one of the honest hands—perhaps of the last one left aboard. But on this point I was soon to be relieved, for, Silver giving a little whistle, a third man strolled up and sat down by the party.

"Dick's square," said Silver.

"Oh, I know'd Dick was square," returned the voice of the coxswain, Israel Hands. "He's no fool, is Dick." And he turned his quid and spat. "But, look here," he went on, "here's what I want to know, Barbecue—how long are we a-going to stand off and on like a blessed bumboat? I've had a'most enough o' Cap'n Smollett; he's hazed me long enough, by thunder! I want to go into that cabin, I do. I want their pickles and wines, and that."

"Israel," said Silver, "your head ain't much account, nor never was. But you're able to hear, I reckon; leastways your ears is big enough. Now, here's what I say—you'll berth forward, and you'll live hard, and you'll speak soft, and you'll keep sober, till I give the word; and you may lay to that, my son."

"Well, I don't say no, do I?" growled the coxswain. "What I say is, when? That's what I say."

"When! by the powers!" cried Silver. "Well, now, if you want to know, I'll tell you when. The last moment I can manage; and that's when. Here's a first-rate seaman, Cap'n Smollett, sails the blessed ship for us. Here's this squire and doctor with a map and such—I don't know where it is, do I? No more do you, says you. Well, then, I mean this squire and doctor shall find the stuff, and help us to get it aboard, by the powers! Then we'll see. If I was sure of you all, sons of double Dutchmen, I'd have Cap'n Smollett navigate us halfway back again before I struck."

"Why, we're all seamen aboard here, I should think," said the lad Dick.

"We're all foc's'le hands, you mean," snapped Silver. "We can steer a course, but who's to set one? That's what all you gentlemen split on, first and last. If I had my way, I'd have Cap'n Smollett work us back into the trades at least; then we'd have no blessed miscalculations and a spoonful of water a day. But I know the sort you are. I'll finish with 'em at the island, as soon's the blunt's on board, and a pity it is. But you're never happy till you're drunk. Split my sides, I've a sick heart to sail with the likes of you!"

"Easy all, Long John," cried Israel. "Who's a-crossin' of you?"

"Why, how many tall ships, think ye, now, have I seen laid aboard? And how many brisk lads drying in the sun at Execution Dock?" cried Silver; "and all for this same hurry and hurry and hurry. You hear me? I seen a thing or two at sea, I have. If you would on'y lay your course, and a p'int to windward, you would ride in carriages, you would. But not you! I know you. You'll have your mouthful of rum to-morrow, and go hang."

"Everybody know'd you was a kind of a chapling, John; but there's others as could hand and steer as well as you," said Israel. "They liked a bit o' fun, they did. They wasn't so high and dry, nohow, but took their fling, like jolly companions, everyone."

"So?" said Silver. "Well, and where are they now? Pew was that sort, and he died a beggar-man. Flint was, and he died of rum at Savannah. Ah, they was a sweet crew, they was! on'y, where are they?"

"But," asked Dick, "when we do lay 'em athwart, what are we to do with 'em, anyhow?"

"There's the man for me!" cried the cook, admiringly. "That's what I call business. Well, what would you think? Put 'em ashore like maroons? That would have been England's way. Or cut 'em down like that much pork? That would have been Flint's or Billy Bones's."

"Billy was the man for that," said Israel. "'Dead men don't bite,' says he. Well, he's dead now, hisself; he knows the long and short on it now; and if ever a rough hand come to port, it was Billy."

"Right you are," said Silver, "rough and ready. But mark you here: I'm an easy man—I'm quite the gentleman, says you; but this time it's serious. Dooty is dooty, mates. I give my vote—death. When I'm in Parlyment, and riding in my coach, I don't want none of these sea-lawyers in the cabin a-coming home, unlooked for, like the devil at prayers. Wait is what I say; but when the time comes, why let her rip!"

"John," cried the coxswain, "you're a man!"

"You'll say so, Israel, when you see," said Silver. "Only one thing I claim—I claim Trelawney. I'll wring his calf's head off his body with these hands. Dick!" he added, breaking off, "You must jump up, like a sweet lad, and get me an apple, to wet my pipe like."

You may fancy the terror I was in! I should have leaped out and run for it, if I had found the strength; but my limbs and heart alike misgave me. I heard Dick begin to rise, and then some one seemingly stopped him, and the voice of Hands exclaimed:

"Oh, stow that! Don't you get sucking of that bilge, John. Let's have a go of the rum."

"Dick," said Silver, "I trust you. I've a gauge on the keg, mind. There's the key; you fill a pannikin and bring it up."

Terrified as I was, I could not help thinking to myself that this must have been how Mr. Arrow got the strong waters that destroyed him.

Dick was gone but a little while, and during his absence Israel spoke straight on in the cook's ear. It was but a word or two that I could catch, and yet I gathered some important news; for, besides other scraps that tended to the same purpose, this whole clause was audible: "Not another man of them'll jine." Hence there were still faithful men on board.

When Dick returned, one after another of the trio took the pannikin and drank—one "To luck," another with a "Here's to old Flint," and Silver himself saying, in a kind of song, "Here's to ourselves, and hold your luff, plenty of prizes and plenty of duff."

Just then a sort of brightness fell upon me in the barrel, and, looking up, I found the moon had risen, and was silvering the mizzen-top and shining white on the luff of the foresail, and almost at the same time the voice on the lookout shouted, "Land ho!"

There was a great rush of feet across the deck. I could hear people tumbling up from the cabin and the foc's'le; and slipping in an instant outside my barrel, I dived behind the foresail, made a double towards the stern, and came out upon the open deck in time to join Hunter and Doctor Livesey in the rush for the weather bow.

There all hands were already congregated. A belt of fog had lifted almost simultaneously with the appearance of the moon. Away to the southwest of us we saw two low hills, about a couple of miles apart, and rising behind one of them a third and higher hill, whose peak was still buried in the fog. All three seemed sharp and conical in figure.

So much I saw almost in a dream, for I had not yet recovered from my horrid fear of a minute or two before. And then I heard the voice of Captain Smollett issuing orders. The *Hispaniola* was laid a couple of points nearer the wind, and now sailed a course that would just clear the island on the east.

"And now, men," said the captain, when all was sheeted home, "has any one of you ever seen that land ahead?"

"I have, sir," said Silver. "I've watered there with a trader I was cook in."

"The anchorage is on the south, behind an islet, I fancy?" asked the captain.

"Yes, sir, Skeleton Island they calls it. It were a main place for pirates once, and a hand we had on board knowed all their names for it. That hill to the nor'ard they calls the Foremast Hill; there are three hills in a row running south'ard—fore, main, and mizzen, sir. But the main—that's the big 'un, with the cloud on it—they usually calls the Spy-glass, by reason of a lookout they kept when they was in the anchorage cleaning; for it's there they cleaned their ships, sir, asking your pardon."

"I have a chart here," said Captain Smollett. "See if that's the place."

Long John's eyes burned in his head as he took the chart, but, by the fresh look of the paper, I knew he was doomed to disappointment. This was not the map we found in Billy Bones's chest, but an accurate copy, complete in all things—names, and heights, and soundings—with the single exception of the red crosses and the written notes. Sharp as must have been his annoyance, Silver had the strength of mind to hide it.

"Yes, sir," said he, "this is the spot, to be sure, and very prettily drawed out. Who might have done that, I wonder? The pirates were too ignorant, I reckon. Ay, here it is: 'Captain Kidd's Anchorage'—just the name my shipmate called it. There's a strong current runs along the south, and then away nor'ard up the west coast. Right you was, sir," said he, "to haul your wind and keep the weather of the island. Leastways, if such was your intention as to enter and careen, and there ain't no better place for that in these waters."

"Thank you, my man," said Captain Smollett. "I'll ask you, later on, to give us a help. You may go."

I was surprised at the coolness with which John avowed his knowledge of the island, and I own I was half-frightened when I saw him drawing nearer to myself. He did not know, to be sure, that I had overheard his council from the apple barrel, and yet I had, by this time, taken such a horror of his cruelty, duplicity, and power, that I could scarce conceal a shudder when he laid his hand upon my arm.

"Ah," said he, "this here is a sweet spot, this island—a sweet spot for a lad to get ashore on. You'll bathe, and you'll climb trees, and you'll hunt goats, you will, and you'll get aloft on them hills like a goat yourself. Why, it makes me young again. I was going to forget my timber leg, I was. It's a pleasant thing to be young, and have ten toes, and you may lay to that. When you want to go a bit of exploring, you just ask old John and he'll put up a snack for you to take along."

And clapping me in the friendliest way upon the shoulder, he hobbled off forward and went below.

Captain Smollett, the squire, and Doctor Livesey were talking together on the quarterdeck, and anxious as I was to tell them my story, I durst not interrupt them openly. While I was still casting about in my thoughts to find some probable excuse, Doctor Livesey called me to his side. He had left his pipe below, and being a slave to tobacco, had meant that I should fetch it; but as soon as I was near enough to speak and not be overheard, I broke out immediately: "Doctor, let me speak. Get the captain and squire down to the cabin, and then make some pretense to send for me. I have terrible news."

The doctor changed countenance a little, but next moment he was master of himself.

"Thank you, Jim," said he, quite loudly; "that was all I wanted to know," as if he had asked me a question.

And with that he turned on his heel and rejoined the other two. They spoke together for a little, and though none of them started, or raised his voice, or so much as whistled, it was plain enough that Doctor Livesey had communicated my request, for the next thing that I heard was the captain giving an order to Job Anderson, and all hands were piped on deck.

"My lads," said Captain Smollett, "I've a word to say to you. This land that we have sighted is the place we have been sailing to. Mr. Trelawney, being a very open-handed gentleman, as we all know, has just asked me a word or two, and as I was able to tell him that every man on board had done his duty, alow and aloft, as I never ask to see it done better, why, he and I and the doctor are going below to the cabin to drink your health and luck, and you'll have grog served out for you to drink our health and luck. I'll tell you what I think of this: I think it handsome. And if you think as I do, you'll give a good sea cheer for the gentleman that does it."

The cheer followed—that was a matter of course—but it rang out so full and hearty, that I confess I could hardly believe these same men were plotting for our blood.

"One more cheer for Cap'n Smollett!" cried Long John, when the first had subsided.

And this also was given with a will.

On the top of that the three gentlemen went below, and not long after, word was sent forward that Jim Hawkins was wanted in the cabin.

I found them all three seated around the table, a bottle of Spanish wine and some raisins before them, and the doctor smoking away, with his wig on his lap, and that, I knew, was a sign that he was agitated. The stern window was open, for it was a warm night, and you could see the moon shining behind on the ship's wake.

"Now, Hawkins," said the squire, "you have something to say. Speak up."

I did as I was bid, and, as short as I could make it, told the whole details of Silver's conversation. Nobody interrupted me till I was done, nor did anyone of the three of them make so much as a movement, but they kept their eyes upon my face from first to last.

"Jim," said Doctor Livesey, "take a seat."

And they made me sit down at a table beside them, poured me out a glass of wine, filled my hands with raisins, and all three, one after the other, and each with a bow, drank my good health, and their service to me, for my luck and courage.

"Now, captain," said the squire, "you were right and I was wrong. I own myself an ass, and I await your orders."

"No more an ass than I, sir," returned the captain. "I never heard of a crew that meant to mutiny but what showed signs before, for any man that had an eye in his head to see the mischief and take steps according. But this crew," he added, "beats me."

"Captain," said the doctor, "with your permission, that's Silver. A very remarkable man."

"He'd look remarkably well from a yardarm, sir," returned the captain. "But this is talk; this don't lead to anything. I see three or four points, and with Mr. Trelawney's permission I'll name them."

"You, sir, are the captain. It is for you to speak," said Mr. Trelawney, grandly.

"First point," began Mr. Smollett, "we must go on because we can't turn back. If I gave the word to turn about, they would rise at once. Second point, we have time before us—at least until this treasure's found. Third point, there are faithful hands. Now, sir, it's got to come to blows sooner or later, and what I propose is to take time by the forelock, as the saying is, and come to blows some fine day when they least expect it. We can count, I take it, on your own home servants, Mr. Trelawney?"

"As upon myself," declared the squire.

"Three," reckoned the captain; "ourselves make seven, counting Hawkins here. Now, about the honest hands?"

"Most likely Trelawney's own men," said the doctor; "those he picked up for himself before he lit on Silver."

"Nay," replied the squire, "Hands was one of mine."

"I did think I could have trusted Hands," added the captain.

"And to think that they're all Englishmen!" broke out the squire. "Sir, I could find it in my heart to blow the ship up."

"Well, gentlemen," said the captain, "the best that I can say is not much. We must lay to, if you please, and keep a bright lookout. It's trying on a man, I know. It would be pleasanter to come to blows. But there's no help for it till we know our men. Lay to and whistle for a wind; that's my view."

"Jim here," said the doctor, "can help us more than anyone. The men are not shy with him and Jim is a noticing lad."

"Hawkins, I put prodigious faith in you," added the squire.

I began to feel pretty desperate at this, for I felt altogether helpless; and yet, by an odd train of circumstances, it was indeed through me that safety came. In the meantime, talk as we pleased, there were only seven out of the twenty-six on whom we knew we could rely, and out of these seven one was a boy, so that the grown men on our side were six to their nineteen.

⌒

Owing to the cant of the vessel, the masts hung far out over the water, and from my perch on the crosstrees I had nothing below me but the surface of the bay. Hands, who was not so far up, was, in consequence, nearer to the ship, and fell between me and the bulwarks. He rose once to the surface in a lather of foam and blood, and then sank again for good. As the water settled, I could see him lying huddled together on the clean, bright sand in the shadow of the vessel's sides. A fish or two whipped past his body. Sometimes, by the quivering of the water, he appeared to move a little, as if he were trying to rise. But he was dead enough, for all that, being both shot and drowned, and was food for fish in the very place where he had designed my slaughter.

I was no sooner certain of this than I began to feel sick, faint, and terrified. The hot blood was running over my back and chest. The dirk, where it had pinned my shoulder to the mast, seemed to burn like a hot iron; yet it was not so much these real sufferings that distressed me, for these, it seemed to me, I could bear without a murmur; it was the horror I had upon my mind of falling from the crosstree into that still, green water beside the body of the coxswain.

I clung with both hands till my nails ached, and I shut my eyes as if to cover up the peril. Gradually my mind came back again, my pulses quieted down to a more natural time, and I was once more in possession of myself.

It was my first thought to pluck forth the dirk; but either it stuck too hard or my nerve failed me, and I desisted with a violent shudder. Oddly enough, that very shudder did the business. The knife, in fact, had come the nearest in the world to missing me altogether; it held me by a mere pinch of skin, and this the shudder tore away. The blood ran down the faster, to be sure, but I was my own master again, and only tacked to the mast by my coat and shirt.

These last I broke through with a sudden jerk, and then regained the deck by the starboard shrouds. For nothing in the world would I have again ventured, shaken as I was, upon the overhanging port shrouds, from which Israel had so lately fallen.

I went below and did what I could for my wound; it pained me a good deal and still bled freely, but it was neither deep nor dangerous, nor did it greatly gall me when I used my arm. Then I looked around me, and as the ship was now, in a sense, my own, I began to think of clearing it from its last passenger—the dead man, O'Brien.

He had pitched, as I have said, against the bulwarks, where he lay like some horrid, ungainly sort of puppet; life-size, indeed, but how different from life's color or life's comeliness! In that position, I could easily have my way with him, and as the habit of tragical adventures had worn off almost all my terror for the dead, I took him by the waist as if he had been a sack of bran, and, with one good heave, tumbled him overboard. He went in with a sounding plunge; the red cap came off, and remained floating on the surface; and as soon as the splash subsided, I could see him and Israel lying side by side, both wavering with the tremulous movement of the water. O'Brien, though still quite a young man, was very bald. There he lay with that bald head across the knees of the man who killed him, and the quick fishes steering to and fro over both.

I was now alone upon the ship; the tide had just turned. The sun was within so few degrees of setting that already the shadow of the pines upon the western shore began to reach right across the anchorage and fall in patterns on the deck. The evening breeze had sprung up, and though it was well warded off by the hill with the two peaks upon the east, the cordage had begun to sing a little softly to itself and the idle sails to rattle to and fro.

I began to see a danger to the ship. The jibs I speedily doused and brought tumbling to the deck, but the mainsail was a harder matter. Of course, when the schooner canted over, the boom had swung outboard, and the cap of it and a foot or two of sail hung even under water. I thought this made it still more dangerous, yet the strain was so heavy that I half feared to meddle. At last I got my knife and cut the halyards. The peak dropped instantly, a great belly of loose canvas floated broad upon the water; and since, pull as I liked, I could not budge the downhaul, that was the extent of what I could accomplish. For the rest, the *Hispaniola* must trust to luck, like myself.

By this time the whole anchorage had fallen into shadow— the last rays, I remember, falling through a glade of the wood, and shining bright as jewels on the flowery mantle of the wreck. It began to be chill, the tide was rapidly fleeting seaward, the schooner settling more and more on her beam-ends.

I scrambled forward and looked over. It seemed shallow enough, and holding the cut hawser in both hands for a last security, I let myself drop softly overboard. The water scarcely reached my waist; the sand was firm and covered with ripple-marks, and I waded ashore in great spirits, leaving the *Hispaniola* on her side, with her mainsail trailing wide upon the surface of the bay. About the same time the sun went fairly down, and the breeze whistled low in the dusk among the tossing pines.

At least, and at last, I was off the sea, nor had I returned thence empty-handed. There lay the schooner, clear at last from buccaneers and ready for our own men to board and get to sea again. I had nothing nearer my fancy than to get home to the stockade and boast of my achievements. Possibly I might be blamed a bit for my truantry, but the recapture of the *Hispaniola* was a clinching answer, and I hoped that even Captain Smollett would confess I had not lost my time.

So thinking, and in famous spirits, I began to set my face homeward for the blockhouse and my companions. I remembered that the most easterly of the rivers which drain into Captain Kidd's anchorage ran from the two-peaked hill upon my left; and I bent my course in that direction that I might pass the stream while it was small. The wood was pretty open, and keeping along the lower spurs, I had soon turned the corner of that hill, and not long after waded to the mid-calf across the watercourse.

This brought me near to where I had encountered Ben Gunn, the maroon, and I walked more circumspectly, keeping an eye on every side. The dusk had come nigh hand completely, and, as I opened out the cleft between the two peaks, I became aware of a wavering glow against the sky, where, as I judged, the man of the island was cooking his supper before a roaring fire. And yet I wondered, in my heart, that he should show himself so careless. For if I could see this radiance, might it not reach the eye of Silver himself where he camped upon the shore among the marshes?

Gradually the night fell blacker; it was all I could do to guide myself even roughly toward my destination; the double hill behind me and the Spy-glass on my right hand loomed faint and fainter, the stars were few and pale, and in the low ground where I wandered I kept tripping among bushes and rolling into sandy pits.

Suddenly a kind of brightness fell about me. I looked up; a pale glimmer of moonbeams had alighted on the summit of the Spy-glass, and soon after I saw something broad and silvery moving low down behind the trees, and knew the moon had risen.

With this to help me, I passed rapidly over what remained to me of my journey; and, sometimes walking, sometimes running, impatiently drew near to the stockade. Yet, as I began to thread the grove that lies before it, I was not so thoughtless but that I slacked my pace and went a trifle warily. It would have been a poor end of my adventures to get shot down by my own party in mistake.

The moon was climbing higher and higher; its light began to fall here and there in masses through the more open districts of the wood, and right in front of me a glow of a different color appeared among the trees. It was red and hot, and now and again it was a little darkened—as it were the embers of a bonfire smoldering.

For the life of me I could not think what it might be.

At last I came right down upon the borders of the clearing. The western end was already steeped in moon-shine; the rest, and the blockhouse itself, still lay in a black shadow, chequered with long, silvery streaks of light. On the other side of the house an immense fire had burned itself into clear embers and shed a steady, red reverberation, contrasting strongly with the mellow paleness of the moon. There was not a soul stirring, nor a sound beside the noises of the breeze.

I stopped, with much wonder in my heart, and perhaps a little terror also. It had not been our way to build great fires; we were, indeed, by the captain's orders, somewhat niggardly of firewood, and I began to fear that something had gone wrong while I was absent.

I stole round by the eastern end, keeping close in shadow, and at a convenient place, where the darkness was thickest, crossed the palisade.

To make assurance surer, I got upon my hands and knees, and crawled, without a sound, toward the corner of the house. As I drew nearer, my heart was suddenly and greatly lightened. It was not a pleasant noise in itself, and I have often complained of it at other times, but just then it was like music to hear my friends snoring together so loud and peaceful in their sleep. The sea-cry of the watch, that beautiful "All's well," never fell more reassuringly on my ear.

In the meantime there was no doubt of one thing; they kept an infamous bad watch. If it had been Silver and his lads that were now creeping in on them, not a soul would have seen daybreak. That was what it was, thought I, to have the captain wounded; and again I blamed myself sharply for leaving them in that danger with so few to mount guard.

By this time I had got to the door and stood up. All was dark within, so that I could distinguish nothing by the eye. As for sounds, there was the steady drone of the snorers, and a small occasional noise, a flickering or pecking that I could in no way account for.

With my arms before me I walked steadily in. I should lie down in my own place (I thought, with a silent chuckle) and enjoy their faces when they found me in the morning. My foot struck something yielding—it was a sleeper's leg, and he turned and groaned, but without awaking.

And then, all of a sudden, a shrill voice broke forth out of the darkness:

"Pieces of eight! pieces of eight! pieces of eight! pieces of eight! pieces of eight!" and so forth, without pause or change, like the clacking of a tiny mill.

Silver's green parrot, Captain Flint! It was she whom I had heard pecking at a piece of bark; it was she, keeping better watch than any human being, who thus announced my arrival with her wearisome refrain. I had no time left me to recover. At the sharp clipping tone of the parrot, the sleepers awoke and sprang up, and with a mighty oath the voice of Silver cried:

"Who goes?"

I turned to run, struck violently against one person, recoiled, and ran full into the arms of a second, who, for his part, closed upon and held me tight.

"Bring a torch, Dick," said Silver, when my capture was thus assured.

And one of the men left the log-house, and presently returned with a lighted brand.

The red glare of the torch lighting up the interior of the blockhouse showed me the worst of my apprehensions realized. The pirates were in possession of the house and stores; there was the cask of cognac, there were the pork and bread, as before; and, what tenfold increased my horror, not a sign of any prisoner. I could only judge that all had perished, and my heart smote me sorely that I had not been there to perish with them.

There were six of the buccaneers, all told; not another man was left alive. Five of them were on their feet, flushed and swollen, suddenly called out of the first sleep of drunkenness. The sixth had only risen upon his elbow; he was deadly pale, and the blood-stained bandage round his head told that he had recently been wounded, and still more recently dressed. I remembered the man who had been shot and run back among the woods in the great attack, and doubted not that this was he.

The parrot sat, preening her plumage, on Long John's shoulder. He himself, I thought, looked somewhat paler and more stern than I was used to. He still wore his fine broadcloth suit in which he had fulfilled his mission, but it was bitterly the worse for wear, daubed with clay and torn with sharp briers of the wood.

"So," said he, "here's Jim Hawkins, shiver my timbers! Dropped in, like, eh? Well, come, I take that friendly."

And thereupon he sat down across the brandy-cask, and began to fill a pipe.

"Give me the loan of a link, Dick," said he; and then, when he had a good light, "That'll do, my lad," he added, "stick the glim in the wood heap; and you, gentlemen, bring yourselves to! You needn't stand up for Mr. Hawkins; he'll excuse you, you may lay to that. And so, Jim"—stopping the tobacco—"here you are, and quite a pleasant surprise for poor old John. I see you were smart when first I set my eyes on you, but this here gets away from me clean, it do."

To all this, as may be well supposed, I made no answer. They had set me with my back against the wall, and I stood there, looking Silver in the face, pluckily enough, I hope, to all outward appearance, but with black despair in my heart.

Silver took a whiff or two of his pipe with great composure, and then ran on again:

"Now, you see, Jim, so be as you are here," says he, "I'll give you a piece of my mind. I've always liked you, I have, for a lad of spirit, and the picter of my own self when I was young and handsome. I always wanted you to jine and take your share, and die a gentleman, and now, my cock, you've got to. Cap'n Smollett's a fine seaman, as I'll own up to any day, but stiff on discipline. 'Dooty is dooty,' says he, and right he is. Just you keep clear of the cap'n. The doctor himself is gone dead again you— 'ungrateful scamp' was what he said; and the short and long of the whole story is about here: You can't go back to your own lot, for they won't have you; and, without you start a third ship's company all by yourself, which might be lonely, you'll have to jine with Cap'n Silver."

So far so good. My friends, then, were still alive, and though I partly believed the truth of Silver's statement, that the cabin party were incensed at me for my desertion, I was more relieved than distressed by what I heard.

"I don't say nothing as to your being in our hands," continued Silver, "though there you are, and you may lay to it. I'm all for argyment; I never seen good come out o' threatening. If you like the service, well, you'll jine; and if you don't, Jim, why, you're free to answer no—free and welcome, shipmate; and if fairer can be said by mortal seaman, shiver my sides!"

"Am I to answer, then?" I asked, with a very tremulous voice. Through all this sneering talk I was made to feel the threat of death that overhung me, and my cheeks burned and my heart beat painfully in my breast.

"Lad," said Silver, "no one's a-pressing of you. Take your bearings. None of us won't hurry you, mate; time goes so pleasant in your company, you see."

"Well," says I, growing a bit bolder, "if I'm to choose, I declare I have a right to know what's what, and why you're here, and where my friends are."

"Wot's wot?" repeated one of the buccaneers, in a deep growl. "Ah, he'd be a lucky one as knowed that!"

"You'll, perhaps, batten down your hatches till you're spoke to, my friend," cried Silver, truculently, to this speaker. And then, in his first gracious tones, he replied to me: "Yesterday morning, Mr. Hawkins," said he, "in the dogwatch, down came Doctor Livesey with a flag of truce. Says he: 'Cap'n Silver, you're sold out. Ship's gone!' Well, maybe we'd been taking a glass, and a song to help it round. I won't say no. Leastways, none of us had looked out. We looked out, and, by thunder! the old ship was gone. I never seen a pack o' fools look fishier; and you may lay to that, if I tells you that I looked the fishiest. 'Well,' says the doctor, 'let's bargain.' We bargained, him and I, and here we are; stores, brandy, blockhouse, the firewood you was thoughtful enough to cut, and, in a manner of speaking, the whole blessed boat, from crosstrees to keelson. As for them, they've tramped; I don't know where's they are."

He drew again quietly at his pipe.

"And lest you should take it into that head of yours," he went on, "that you was included in the treaty, here's the last word that was said: 'How many are you,' says I, 'to leave?' 'Four,' says he—'four, and one of us wounded. As for that boy, I don't know where he is, confound him,' says he, 'nor I don't much care. We're about sick of him.' These was his words."

"Is that all?" I asked.

"Well, it's all you're to hear, my son," returned Silver.

"And now I am to choose?"

"And now you are to choose, and you may lay to that," said Silver.

"Well," said I, "I am not such a fool but I know pretty well what I have to look for. Let the worst come to the worst, it's little I care. I've seen too many die since I fell in with you. But there's a thing or two I have to tell you," I said, and by this time I was quite excited; "and the first is this: Here you are, in a bad way; ship lost, treasure lost, men lost; your whole business gone to wreck; and if you want to know who did it—it was I! I was in the apple barrel the night we sighted land, and I heard you, John, and you, Dick Johnson, and Hands, who is now at the bottom of the sea, and told every word you said before the hour was out. And as for the schooner, it was I who cut her cable, and it was I who killed the men you had aboard of her, and it was I who brought her where you'll never see her more, not one of you. The laugh's on my side; I've had the top of this business from the first; I no more fear you than I fear a fly. Kill me, if you please, or spare me. But one thing I'll say, and no more; if you spare me, bygones are bygones, and when you fellows are in court for piracy, I'll save you all I can. It is for you to choose. Kill another and do yourselves no good, or spare me and keep a witness to save you from the gallows."

I stopped, for, I tell you, I was out of breath, and, to my wonder, not a man of them moved, but all sat staring at me like as many sheep. And while they were still staring I broke out again:

"And now, Mr. Silver," I said, "I believe you're the best man here, and if things go to the worst, I'll take it kind of you to let the doctor know the way I took it."

"I'll bear it in mind," said Silver, with an accent so curious that I could not, for the life of me, decide whether he were laughing at my request or had been favorably affected by my courage.

"I'll put one to that," cried the old mahogany-faced seaman—Morgan by name—whom I had seen in Long John's public-house upon the quays of Bristol. "It was him that knowed Black Dog."

"Well, and see here," added the sea-cook, "I'll put another again to that, by thunder! for it was this same boy that faked the chart from Billy Bones. First and last we've split upon Jim Hawkins!"

"Then here goes!" said Morgan, with an oath.

And he sprang up, drawing his knife as if he had been twenty.

"Avast, there!" cried Silver. "Who are you, Tom Morgan? Maybe you thought you were captain here, perhaps. By the powers, but I'll teach you better! Cross me and you'll go where many a good man's gone before you, first and last, these thirty year back—some to the yardarm, shiver my sides! and some by the board, and all to feed the fishes. There's never a man looked me between the eyes and seen a good day a'terward, Tom Morgan, you may lay to that."

Morgan paused, but a hoarse murmur rose from the others.

"Tom's right," said one.

"I stood hazing long enough from one," added another. "I'll be hanged if I'll be hazed by you, John Silver."

"Did any of you gentlemen want to have it out with me?" roared Silver, bending far forward from his position on the keg, with his pipe still glowing in his right hand. "Put a name on what you're at; you ain't dumb, I reckon. Him that wants shall get it. Have I lived this many years to have a son of a rum puncheon cock his hat athwart my hawser at the latter end of it? You know the way; you're all gentlemen o' fortune, by your account. Well, I'm ready. Take a cutlass, him that dares, and I'll see the color of his inside, crutch and all, before that pipe's empty."

Not a man stirred; not a man answered.

"That's your sort, is it?" he added, returning his pipe to his mouth. "Well, you're a gay lot to look at, any way. Not worth much to fight, you ain't. P'r'aps you can understand King George's English. I'm cap'n here by 'lection. I'm cap'n here because I'm the best man by a long sea-mile. You won't fight, as gentlemen o' fortune should; then, by thunder, you'll obey, and you may lay to it! I like that boy, now; I never seen a better boy than that. He's more a man than any pair of rats of you in this here house, and what I say is this: Let me see him that'll lay a hand on him—that's what I say, and you may lay to it."

There was a long pause after this. I stood straight up against the wall, my heart still going like a sledgehammer, but with a ray of hope now shining in my bosom. Silver leant back against the wall, his arms crossed, his pipe in the corner of his mouth, as calm as though he had been in church; yet his eye kept wandering furtively, and he kept the tail of it on his unruly followers. They, on their part, drew gradually together toward the far end of the blockhouse, and the low hiss of their whispering sounded in my ears continuously, like a stream. One after another they would look up, and the red light of the torch would fall for a second on their nervous faces; but it was not toward me, it was toward Silver that they turned their eyes.

"You seem to have a lot to say," remarked Silver, spitting far into the air. "Pipe up and let me hear it, or lay to."

"Ax your pardon, sir," returned one of the men; "you're pretty free with some of the rules, maybe you'll kindly keep an eye upon the rest. This crew's dissatisfied; this crew don't vally bullying a marlinspike; this crew has its rights like other crews, I'll make so free as that; and by your own rules I take it we can talk together. I ax your pardon, sir, acknowledging you for to be capting at this present, but I claim my right and steps outside for a council."

And with an elaborate sea-salute this fellow, a long, ill-looking, yellow-eyed man of five-and-thirty, stepped coolly toward the door and disappeared out of the house. One after another the rest followed his example, each making a salute as he passed, each adding some apology. "According to rules," said one. "Foc's'le council," said Morgan. And so with one remark or another, all marched out and left Silver and me alone with the torch.

The sea-cook instantly removed his pipe.

"Now, look you here, Jim Hawkins," he said in a steady whisper that was no more than audible, "you're within half a plank of death and, what's a long sight worse, of torture. They're going to throw me off. But you mark, I stand by you through thick and thin. I didn't mean to; no, not till you spoke up. I was about desperate to lose that much blunt, and be hanged into the bargain. But I see you was the right sort. I says to myself: You stand by Hawkins, John, and Hawkins'll stand by you. You're his last card, and by the living thunder, John, he's yours! Back to back, says I. You save your witness and he'll save your neck!"

I began dimly to understand.

"You mean all's lost?" I asked.

"Ay, by gum, I do!" he answered. "Ship gone, neck gone— that's the size of it. Once I looked into that bay, Jim Hawkins, and seen no schooner—well, I'm tough, but I gave out. As for that lot and their council, mark me, they're outright fools and cowards. I'll save your life—if so be as I can—from them. But see here, Jim—tit for tat—you save Long John from swinging."

I was bewildered; it seemed a thing so hopeless he was asking—he, the old buccaneer, the ringleader throughout.

"What I can do, that I'll do," I said.

"It's a bargain!" cried Long John. "You speak up plucky, and by thunder, I've a chance."

He hobbled to the torch, where it stood propped among the firewood, and took a fresh light to his pipe.

"Understand me, Jim," he said, returning. "I've a head on my shoulders, I have. I'm on squire's side now. I know you've got that ship safe somewheres. How you done it I don't know, but safe it is. I guess Hands and O'Brien turned soft. I never much believed in neither of them. Now you mark me. I ask no questions, nor I won't let others. I know when a game's up, I do; and I know a lad that's stanch. Ah, you that's young—you and me might have done a power of good together!"

He drew some cognac from the cask into a tin cannikin.

"Will you taste, messmate?" he asked, and when I had refused, "Well, I'll take a drain myself, Jim," said he. "I need a caulker, for there's trouble on hand. And, talking o' trouble, why did that doctor give me the chart, Jim?"

My face expressed a wonder so unaffected that he saw the needlessness of further questions.

"Ah, well, he did, though," said he. "And there's something under that, no doubt—something, surely, under that, Jim—bad or good."

And he took another swallow of the brandy, shaking his great fair head like a man who looks forward to the worst.

# The Atrocious Life of Charles Gibbs

## *Charles Ellms*

This atrocious and cruel pirate, when very young, became addicted to vices uncommon in youths of his age, and so far from the gentle reproof and friendly admonition, or the more severe chastisement of a fond parent having its intended effect, it seemed to render him still worse, and to incline him to repay those whom he ought to have esteemed as his best friends and who had manifested so much regard for his welfare with ingratitude and neglect. His infamous career and ignominious death on the gallows; brought down the "grey hairs of his parents in sorrow to the grave." The poignant affliction which the infamous crimes of children bring upon their relatives ought to be one of the most effective persuasions for them to refrain from vice.

Charles Gibbs was born in the state of Rhode Island in 1794; his parents and connexions were of the first respectability. When at school, he was very apt to learn, but so refractory and sulky that neither the birch nor good counsel made any impression on him, and he was expelled from the school.

He was now made to labor on a farm; but having a great antipathy to work, when about fifteen years of age, feeling a great inclination to roam, and like too many unreflecting youths of that age, a great fondness for the sea, he in opposition to the friendly counsel of his parents privately left them and entered on board the United States sloop-of-war, *Hornet,* and was in the action when she captured the British sloop-of-war *Peacock,* off the coast of Pernambuco. Upon the return of the *Hornet* to the United States, her brave commander, Capt. Lawrence, was promoted for his gallantry to the command of the unfortunate *Chesapeake,* and to which he was followed by young Gibbs, who took a very distinguished part in the engagement with the *Shannon,* which resulted in the death of Lawrence and the capture of the *Chesapeake.* Gibbs states that while on board the *Chesapeake* the crew, previous to the action, were almost in a state of mutiny, growing out of the non-payment of the prize money, and that the address of Capt. Lawrence was received by them with coldness and murmurs.

After the engagement, Gibbs became, with the survivors of the crew, a prisoner of war, and as such was confined in Dartmoor prison until exchanged.

After his exchange, he returned to Boston, where having determined to abandon the sea, he applied to his friends in Rhode Island to assist him in commencing business; they accordingly lent him one thousand dollars as a capital to begin with. He opened a grocery in Ann Street, near what was then called the Tin Pot, a place full of abandoned women and dissolute fellows. As he dealt chiefly in liquor, and had a "License to retail Spirits," his drunkery was thronged with customers. But he sold his groceries chiefly to loose girls who paid him in their coin, which, although it answered his purpose, would neither buy him goods or pay his rent, and he found his stock rapidly dwindling away without his receiving any cash to replenish it. By dissipation and inattention his new business proved unsuccessful to him. He resolved to abandon it and again try the sea for a subsistence. With a hundred dollars in his pocket, the remnant of his property, he embarked in the ship *John,* for Buenos Ayres, and his means being exhausted soon after his arrival there, he entered on board a Buenos Ayrean privateer and sailed on a cruise. A quarrel between the officers and crew in regard to the division of prize money led eventually to a mutiny; and the mutineers gained the ascendancy, took possession of the vessel, landed the crew on the coast of Florida, and steered for the West Indies, with hearts resolved to make their fortunes at all hazards, and where in a short time, more than twenty vessels were captured by them and nearly Four Hundred Human Beings Murdered!

Havana was the resort of these pirates to dispose of their plunder; and Gibbs sauntered about this place with impunity and was acquainted in all the out-of-the-way and bye places of that hot bed of pirates, the Regla. He and his comrades even lodged in the very houses with many of the American officers who were sent out to take them. He was acquainted with many of the officers and was apprised of all their intended movements before they left the harbor. On one occasion, the American ship *Caroline* was captured by two of their piratical vessels off Cape Antonio. They were busily engaged in landing the cargo when the British sloop-of-war, *Jearus,* hove in sight and sent her barges to attack them. The pirates defended themselves for some time behind a small four gun battery which they had erected, but in the end were forced to abandon their own vessel and the prize and fly to the mountains for safety. The *Jearus* found here twelve vessels burnt to the water's edge, and it was satisfactorily ascertained that their crews, amounting to one hundred and fifty persons, had been murdered. The crews, if it was thought not necessary otherways to dispose of them, were sent adrift in their boats, and frequently without any thing on which they could subsist a single day; nor were all so fortunate thus to escape. "Dead men can tell no tales," was a common saying among them; and as soon as a ship's crew were taken, a short consultation was held; and if it was the opinion of a majority that it would be better to take life than to spare it, a single nod or wink from the captain was sufficient; regardless of age or sex, all entreaties for mercy were then made in vain; they possessed not the tender feelings to be operated upon by the shrieks and expiring groans of the devoted victims! There was a strife among them, who with his own hands could despatch the greatest number, and in the shortest period of time.

Without any other motives than to gratify their hellish propensities (in their intoxicated moments), blood was not unfrequently and unnecessarily shed, and many widows and orphans probably made, when the lives of the unfortunate victims might have been spared, and without the most distant prospect of any evil consequences (as regarded themselves), resulting therefrom.

Gibbs states that sometime in the course of the year 1819, he left Havana and came to the United States, bringing with him about $30,000. He passed several weeks in the city of New York, and then went to Boston, whence he took passage for Liverpool in the ship *Emerald*. Before he sailed, however, he has squandered a large part of his money by dissipation and gambling. He remained in Liverpool a few months, and then returned to Boston. His residence in Liverpool at that time is satisfactorily ascertained from another source besides his own confession. A female now in New York was well acquainted with him there, where, she says, he lived like a gentleman, with apparently abundant means of support. In speaking of his acquaintance with this female he says, "I fell in with a woman, who I thought was all virtue, but she deceived me, and I am sorry to say that a heart that never felt abashed at scenes of carnage and blood was made a child of for a time by her, and I gave way to dissipation to drown the torment. How often, when the fumes of liquor have subsided, have I thought of my good and affectionate parents, and of their Godlike advice! But when the little monitor began to move within me, I immediately seized the cup to hide myself from myself, and drank until the sense of intoxication was renewed. My friends advised me to behave myself like a man, and promised me their assistance, but the demon still haunted me, and I spurned their advice."

In 1826, he revisited the United States, and hearing of the war between Brazil and the Republic of Buenos Ayres, sailed from Boston in the brig *Hitty*, of Portsmouth, with a determination, as he states, of trying his fortune in defence of a republican government. Upon his arrival he made himself known to Admiral Brown, and communicated his desire to join their navy. The admiral accompanied him to the Governor, and a Lieutenant's commission being given him, he joined a ship of thirty-four guns called the *Twenty Fifth of May*. "Here," says Gibbs, "I found Lieutenant Dodge, an old acquaintance, and a number of other persons with whom I had sailed. When the Governor gave me the commission he told me they wanted no cowards in their navy, to which I replied that I thought he would have no apprehension of my cowardice or skill when he became acquainted with me. He thanked me, and said he hoped he should not be deceived; upon which we drank to his health and to the success of the Republic. He then presented me with a sword, and told me to wear that as my companion through the doubtful struggle in which the republic was engaged. I told him I never would disgrace it, so long as I had a nerve in my arm. I remained on board the ship in the capacity of 5th Lieutenant for about four months, during which time we had a number of skirmishes with the enemy. Having succeeded in gaining the confidence of Admiral Brown, he put me in command of a privateer schooner, mounting two long 24-pounders and 46 men. I sailed from Buenos Ayres, made two good cruises, and returned safely to port. I then bought one half of a new Baltimore schooner and sailed again, but was captured seven days out, and carried into Rio Janeiro, where the Brazilians paid me my change. I remained there until peace took place, then returned to Buenos Ayres, and thence to New York.

"After the lapse of about a year, which I passed in travelling from place to place, the war between France and Algiers attracted my attention. Knowing that the French commerce presented a fine opportunity for plunder, I determined to embark for Algiers and offer my services to the Dey. I accordingly took passage from New York in the *Sally Ann*, belonging to Bath, landed at Barcelona, crossed to Port Mahon, and endeavored to make my way to Algiers. The vigilance of the French fleet prevented the accomplishment of my design, and I proceeded to Tunis. There, finding it unsafe to attempt a journey to Algiers across the desert, I amused myself with contemplating the ruins of Carthage, and reviving my recollections of her war with the Romans. I afterwards took passage to Marseilles, and thence to Boston."

An instance of the most barbarous and cold-blooded murder of which the wretched Gibbs gives an account in the course of his confessions, is that of an innocent and beautiful female of about 17 or 18 years of age! She was with her parents a passenger on board a Dutch ship, bound from Curracoa to Holland; there were a number of other passengers, male and female, on board, all of whom except the young lady above-mentioned were put to death; her unfortunate parents were inhumanly butchered before her eyes, and she was doomed to witness the agonies and to hear the expiring, heart-piercing groans of those whom she held most dear, and on whom she depended for protection! The life of their wretched daughter was spared for the most nefarious purposes—she was taken by the pirates to the west end of Cuba, where they had a rendezvous with a small fort that mounted four guns—here she was confined about two months, and where, as has been said by the murderer Gibbs, "she received such treatment, the bare recollection of which causes me to shudder!" At the expiration of the two months she was taken by the pirates on board of one of their vessels, and among whom a consultation was soon after held, which resulted in the conclusion that it would be necessary for their own personal safety to put her to death! And to her a fatal dose of poison was accordingly administered, which soon proved fatal! when her pure and immortal spirit took its flight to that God, whom, we believe, will avenge her wrongs! Her lifeless body was then committed to the deep by two of the merciless wretches with as much unconcern as if it had been that of the meanest brute! Gibbs persists in the declaration that in this horrid transaction he took no part, that such was his pity for this poor ill-fated female that he interceded for her life so long as he could do it with safety to his own!

Gibbs in his last visit to Boston remained there but a few days, when he took passage to New Orleans, and there entered as one of the crew on board the brig *Vineyard;* and for assisting in the murder of the unfortunate captain and mate of which he was justly condemned, and the awful sentence of death passed upon him! The particulars of the bloody transaction (agreeable to the testimony of Dawes and Brownrigg, the two principal witnesses), are as follows: The brig *Vineyard,* Capt. William Thornby, sailed from New Orleans about the 9th of November, for Philadelphia, with a cargo of 112 bales of cotton, 113 hhds. sugar, 54 casks of molasses and 54,000 dollars in specie. Besides the captain there were on board the brig William Roberts, mate, six seamen shipped at New Orleans, and the cook. Robert Dawes, one of the crew, states on examination that when, about five days out, he was told that there was money on board, Charles Gibbs, E. Church and the steward then determined to take possession of the brig. They asked James Talbot, another of the crew, to join them. He said no, as he did not believe there was money in the vessel. They concluded to kill the captain and mate, and if Talbot and John Brownrigg would not join them, to kill them also. The next night they talked of doing it, and got their clubs ready. Dawes dared not say a word, as they declared they would kill him if he did; as they did not agree about killing Talbot and Brownrigg, two shipmates, it was put off. They next concluded to kill the captain and mate on the night of November 22, but did not get ready. But, on the night of the 23rd, between twelve and one o'clock, as Dawes was at the helm, saw the steward come up with a light and a knife in his hand; he dropt the light and seizing the pump break, struck the captain with it over the head or back of the neck; the captain was sent forward by the blow, and halloed, oh! and murder! once; he was then seized by Gibbs and the cook, one by the head and the other by the heels, and thrown overboard. Atwell and Church stood at the companion way, to strike down the mate when he should come up. As he came up and enquired what was the matter they struck him over the head—he ran back into the cabin, and Charles Gibbs followed him down; but as it was dark, he could not find him—Gibbs came on deck for the light, with which he returned. Dawes' light being taken from him, he could not see to steer, and he in consequence left the helm, to see what was going on below. Gibbs found the mate and seized him, while Atwell and Church came down and struck him with a pump break and a club; he was then dragged upon deck; they called for Dawes to come to them, and as he came up the mate seized his hand, and gave him a death gripe! Three of them then hove him overboard, but which three

boat, they threw overboard a trunk of clothes and a great deal of money, in all about 5,000 dollars—the jolly boat foundered; they saw the boat fill, and heard them cry out, and saw them clinging to the masts—they went ashore on Barron Island, and buried the money in the sand, but very lightly. Soon after they met with a gunner, whom they requested to conduct them where they could get some refreshments. They were by him conducted to Johnson's (the only man living on the island), where they staid all night— Dawes went to bed at about 10 o'clock—Jack Brownrigg set up with Johnson, and in the morning told Dawes that he had told Johnson all about the murder. Johnson went in the morning with the steward for the clothes, which were left on the top of the place where they buried the money, but does not believe they took away the money.

The prisoners, (Gibbs and Wansley), were brought to trial at the February term of the United States Court, holden in the city of New York; when the foregoing facts being satisfactorily proved, they were pronounced guilty, and on the 11th March last, the awful sentence of the law was passed upon them in the following affecting and impressive manner—The Court opened at 11 o'clock, Judge Betts presiding. A few minutes after that hour, Mr. Hamilton, District Attorney, rose and said—May it please the Court, Thomas J. Wansley, the prisoner at the bar, having been tried by a jury of his country, and found guilty of the murder of Captain Thornby, I now move that the sentence of the Court be pronounced upon that verdict.

*By the Court.* Thomas J. Wansley, you have heard what has been said by the District Attorney—by the Grand Jury of the

South District of New York, you have been arraigned for the wilful murder of Captain Thornby, of the brig *Vineyard;* you have been put upon your trial, and after a patient and impartial hearing, you have been found Guilty. The public prosecutor now moves for judgment on that verdict; have you any thing to say, why the sentence of the law should not be passed upon you?

*Thomas J. Wansley.* I will say a few words, but it is perhaps of no use. I have often understood that there is a great deal of difference in respect of color, and I have seen it in this Court. Dawes and Brownrigg were as guilty as I am, and these witnesses have tried to fasten upon me greater guilt than is just, for their life has been given to them. You have taken the blacks from their own country, to bring them here to treat them ill. I have seen this. The witnesses, the jury, and the prosecuting Attorney consider me more guilty than Dawes, to condemn me—for otherwise the law must have punished him; he should have had the same verdict, for he was a perpetrator in the conspiracy. Notwithstanding my participating, they have sworn falsely for the purpose of taking my life; they would not even inform the Court, how I gave information of money being on board; they had the biggest part of the money, and have sworn falsely. I have said enough. I will say no more.

*By the Court.* The Court will wait patiently and hear all you have to say; if you have any thing further to add, proceed.

Wansley then proceeded: In the first place, I was the first to ship on board the *Vineyard* at New Orleans, I knew nobody; I saw the money come on board. The judge that first examined me did not take my deposition down correctly. When talking with the crew on board, they said the brig was an old craft, and when we arrived at Philadelphia, we all agreed to leave her. It was mentioned to me that there was plenty of money on board. Henry Atwell said, "Let's have it." I knew no more of this for some days. Atwell came to me again and asked, "What think you of taking the money." I thought it was a joke, and paid no attention to it. The next day he said they had determined to take the brig and money, and that they were the strongest party, and would murder the officers, and he that informed should suffer with them. I knew Church in Boston, and in a joke asked him how it was made up in the ship's company; his reply, that it was he and Dawes. There was no arms on board as was ascertained; the conspiracy was known to the whole company, and had I informed, my life would have been taken, and though I knew if I was found out my life would be taken by law, which is the same thing, so I did not inform. I have committed murder and I know I must die for it.

*By the Court.* If you wish to add any thing further you will still be heard.

*Wansley.* No sir, I believe I have said enough.

The District Attorney rose and moved for judgment on Gibbs, in the same manner as in the case of Wansley, and the Court having addressed Gibbs in similar terms, concluded by asking what he had to say why the sentence of the law should not now be passed upon him.

Charles Gibbs said: I wish to state to the Court, how far I am guilty and how far I am innocent in this transaction. When I left New Orleans, I was a stranger to all on board, except Dawes and Church. It was off Tortugas that Atwell first told me there was money on board, and proposed to me to take possession of the brig. I refused at that time. The conspiracy was talked of for some days, and at last I agreed that I would join. Brownrigg, Dawes, Church, and the whole agreed that they would. A few days after, however, having thought of the affair, I mentioned to Atwell what a dreadful thing it was to take a man's life, and commit piracy, and recommended him to "abolish," their plan. Atwell and Dawes remonstrated with me; I told Atwell that if ever he would speak of the subject again, I would break his nose. Had I kept to my resolution I would not have been brought here to receive my sentence. It was three days afterwards that the murder was committed. Brownrigg agreed to call up the captain from the cabin, and this man, (pointing to Wansley,) agreed to strike the first blow. The captain was struck and I suppose killed, and I lent a hand to throw him overboard. But for the murder of the mate, of which I have been found guilty, I am innocent—I had nothing to do with that. The mate was murdered by Dawes and Church; that I am innocent of this I commit my soul to that God who will judge all flesh—who will judge all murderers and false swearers, and the wicked who deprive the innocent of his right. I have nothing more to say.

*By the Court.* Thomas J. Wansley and Charles Gibbs, the Court has listened to you patiently and attentively; and although you have said something in your own behalf, yet the Court has heard nothing to affect the deepest and most painful duty that he who presides over a public tribunal has to perform.

You, Thomas J. Wansley, conceive that a different measure of justice has been meted out to you, because of your color. Look back upon your whole course of life; think of the laws under which you have lived, and you will find that to white or black, to free or bond, there is no ground for your allegations; that they are not supported by truth or justice. Admit that Brownrigg and Dawes have sworn falsely; admit that Dawes was concerned with you; admit that Brownrigg is not innocent; admit, in relation to both, that they are guilty, the whole evidence has proved beyond a doubt that you are guilty; and your own words admit that you were an active agent in perpetrating this horrid crime. Two fellow beings who confided in you, and in their perilous voyage called in your assistance, yet you, without reason or provocation, have maliciously taken their lives.

If, peradventure, there was the slightest foundation for a doubt of your guilt in the mind of the Court, judgment would be arrested, but there is none; and it now remains to the Court to pronounce the most painful duty that devolves upon a civil magistrate. The Court is persuaded of your guilt; it can form no other opinion. Testimony has been heard before the Court and Jury—from that we must form our opinion. We must proceed upon testimony, ascertain facts by evidence of witnesses, on which we must inquire, judge, and determine as to guilt or innocence by that evidence alone. You have been found guilty. You now stand for the last time before an earthly tribunal, and by your own acknowledgments, the sentence of the law falls just on your heads. When men in ordinary cases come under the penalty of the law there is generally some palliative—something to warm the sympathy of the Court and Jury. Men may be led astray, and under the influence of passion have acted under some long smothered resentment, suddenly awakened by the force of circumstances, depriving him of reason, and then they may take the life of a fellow being. Killing, under that kind of excitement, might possibly awaken some sympathy, but that was not your case; you had no provocation. What offence had Thornby or Roberts committed against you? They entrusted themselves with you, as able and trustworthy citizens; confiding implicitly in you; no one act of theirs, after a full examination, appears to have been offensive to you; yet for the purpose of securing the money you coolly determined to take their lives—you slept and deliberated over the act; you were tempted on, and yielded; you entered into the conspiracy, with cool and determined calculation to deprive two human beings of their lives, and it was done.

You, Charles Gibbs, have said that you are not guilty of the murder of Roberts; but were you not there, strongly instigating the murderers on, and without stretching out a hand to save him? It is murder as much to stand by and encourage the deed as to stab with a knife, strike with a hatchet, or shoot with a pistol. It is not only murder in law, but in your own feelings and in your own conscience. Notwithstanding all this, I cannot believe that your feelings are so callous, so wholly callous, that your own minds do not melt when you look back upon the unprovoked deeds of yourselves, and those confederated with you.

You are American citizens—this country affords means of instruction to all: Your appearance and your remarks have added evidence that you are more than ordinarily intelligent; that your education has enabled you to participate in the advantages of information open to all classes. The Court will believe that when you were young you looked with strong aversion on the course of life of the wicked. In early life, in boyhood, when you heard of the conduct of men who engaged in robbery—nay more, when you heard of cold-blooded murder—how you must have shrunk from the recital. Yet now, after having participated in the advantages of education, after having arrived at full maturity, you stand here as robbers and murderers.

It is a perilous employment of life that you have followed; in this way of life the most enormous crimes that man can commit are *murder and piracy*. With what detestation would you in early life have looked upon the man who would have raised his hand against his officer, or have committed piracy! Yet now you both stand here murderers and pirates, tried and found guilty—you Wansley of the murder of your Captain, and you, Gibbs, of the murder of your Mate. The evidence has convicted you of rising in mutiny against the master of the vessel, for that alone, the law is *death!*—of murder and robbery on the high seas, for that crime, the law adjudges *death*—of destroying the vessel and embezzling the cargo, even for scuttling and burning the vessel alone the law is *death;* yet of all these the evidence has convicted you, and it only remains now for the Court to pass the sentence of the law. It is, that you, Thomas J. Wansley and Charles Gibbs, be taken hence to the place of confinement, there to remain in close custody, that thence you be taken to the place of execution, and on the 22nd April next, between the hours of 10 and 4 o'clock, you be both publicly hanged by the neck until you are *dead*—and that your bodies be given to the College of Physicians and Surgeons for dissection.

The Court added that the only thing discretionary with it was the time of execution; it might have ordered that you should instantly have been taken from the stand to the scaffold, but the sentence has been deferred to as distant a period as prudent—six weeks. But this time has not been granted for the purpose of giving you any hope for pardon or commutation of the sentence—just as sure as you live till the twenty-second of April, as surely you will suffer death—therefore indulge not a hope that this sentence will be changed!

The Court then spoke of the terror in all men of death!—how they cling to life whether in youth, manhood or old age. What an awful thing it is to die! How in the perils of the sea, when rocks or storms threaten the loss of the vessel and the lives of all on board, how the crew will labor, night and day, in the hope of escaping shipwreck and death! alluded to the tumult, bustle and confusion of battle—yet even there the hero clings to life. The Court adverted not only to the certainty of their coming doom on earth, but to *think of hereafter*—that they should seriously think and reflect of their *future state!* that they would be assisted in their devotions no doubt, by many pious men.

When the Court closed, Charles Gibbs asked if, during his imprisonment, his friends would be permitted to see him. The Court answered that that lay with the Marshal, who then said that no difficulty would exist on that score. The remarks of the Prisoners were delivered in a strong, full-toned and unwavering voice, and they both seemed perfectly resigned to the fate which inevitably awaited them. While Judge Betts was delivering his address to them, Wansley was deeply affected and shed tears—but Gibbs gazed with a steady and unwavering eye, and no sign betrayed the least emotion of his heart. After his condemnation, and during his confinement, his frame became somewhat enfeebled, his face paler, and his eyes more sunken; but the air of his bold, enterprising, and desperate mind still remained. In his narrow cell, he seemed more like an object of pity than vengeance—was affable and communicative, and when he smiled, exhibited so mild and gentle a countenance that no one would take him to be a villain. His conversation was concise and pertinent, and his style of illustration quite original.

Gibbs was married in Buenos Ayres, where he has a child now living. His wife is dead. By a singular concurrence of circumstances, the woman with whom he became acquainted in Liverpool, and who is said at that time to have borne a decent character, was lodged in the same prison with himself. During his confinement he wrote her two letters—one of them is subjoined, to gratify the perhaps innocent curiosity which is naturally felt to know the peculiarities of a man's mind and feelings under such circumstances, and not for the purpose of intimating a belief that he was truly penitent. The reader will be surprised with the apparent readiness with which he made quotations from Scripture.

"Bellevue Prison, March 20, 1831.

"It is with regret that I take my pen in hand to address you with these few lines, under the great embarrassment of my feelings placed within these gloomy walls, my body bound with chains, and under the awful sentence of death! It is enough to throw the strongest mind into gloomy prospects! but I find that

Jesus Christ is sufficient to give consolation to the most despairing soul. For he saith that he that cometh to me I will in no ways cast out. But it is impossible to describe unto you the horror of my feelings. My breast is like the tempestuous ocean, raging in its own shame, harrowing up the bottom of my soul! But I look forward to that serene calm when I shall sleep with Kings and Counsellors of the earth. There the wicked cease from troubling, and there the weary are at rest! There the prisoners rest together—they hear not the voice of the oppressor; and I trust that there my breast will not be ruffled by the storm of sin—for the thing which I greatly feared has come upon me. I was not in safety, neither had I rest; yet trouble came. It is the Lord, let him do what seemeth to him good. When I saw you in Liverpool, and a peaceful calm wafted across both our breasts, and justice no claim upon us, little did I think to meet you in the gloomy walls of a strong prison, and the arm of justice stretched out with the sword of law, awaiting the appointed period to execute the dreadful sentence. I have had a fair prospect in the world, at last it budded, and brought forth the gallows. I am shortly to mount that scaffold, and to bid adieu to this world, and all that was ever dear to my breast. But I trust when my body is mounted on the gallows high, the heavens above will smile and pity me. I hope that you will reflect on your past, and fly to that Jesus who stands with open arms to receive you. Your character is lost, it is true. When the wicked turneth from the wickedness that they have committed, they shall save their soul alive.

"Let us imagine for a moment that we see the souls standing before the awful tribunal, and we hear its dreadful sentence, depart ye cursed into everlasting fire. Imagine you hear the awful lamentations of a soul in hell. It would be enough to melt your heart, if it was as hard as adamant. You would fall upon your knees and plead for God's mercy, as a famished person would for food, or as a dying criminal would for a pardon. We soon, very soon, must go the way whence we shall ne'er return. Our names will be struck off the records of the living, and enrolled in the vast catalogues of the dead. But may it ne'er be numbered with the damned. I hope it will please God to set you at your liberty, and that you may see the sins and follies of your life past. I shall now close my letter with a few words which I hope you will receive as from a dying man; and I hope that every important truth of this letter may sink deep in your heart, and be a lesson to you through life.

> *Rising griefs distress my soul,*
> *And tears on tears successive roll—*
> *For many an evil voice is near,*
> *To chide my woes and mock my fear—*
> *And silent memory weeps alone,*
> *O'er hours of peace and gladness known.*

"I still remain your sincere friend, Charles Gibbs."

In another letter which the wretched Gibbs wrote after his condemnation, to one who had been his early friend, he writes as follows: "Alas! it is now, and not until now, that I have become sensible of my wicked life, from my childhood, and the enormity of the crime for which I must shortly suffer an ignominious death!—I would to God that I never had been born, or that I had died in my infancy!—the hour of reflection has indeed come, but come too late to prevent justice from cutting me off—my mind recoils with horror at the thoughts of the unnatural deeds of which I have been guilty!—my repose rather prevents than affords me relief, as my mind, while I slumber, is constantly disturbed by frightful dreams of my approaching awful dissolution!"

On Friday, April twenty-second, Gibbs and Wansley paid the penalty of their crimes. Both prisoners arrived at the gallows about twelve o'clock, accompanied by the marshal, his aids, and some twenty or thirty United States' marines. Two clergymen attended them to the fatal spot, where everything being in readiness, and the ropes adjusted about their necks, the Throne of Mercy was fervently addressed in their behalf. Wansley then prayed earnestly himself, and afterwards joined in singing a hymn. These exercises concluded, Gibbs addressed the spectators nearly as follows:

"My dear friends,

"My crimes have been heinous—and although I am now about to suffer for the murder of Mr. Roberts, I solemnly declare my innocence of the transaction. It is true, I stood by and saw the fatal deed done, and stretched not forth my arm to save him; the technicalities of the law believe me guilty of the charge—but in the presence of my God—before whom I shall be in a few minutes—I declare I did not murder him.

"I have made a full and frank confession to Mr. Hopson, which probably most of my hearers present have already read; and should any of the friends of those whom I have been accessary to, or engaged in the murder of, be now present, before my Maker I beg their forgiveness—it is the only boon I ask—and as

I hope for pardon through the blood of Christ, surely this request will not be withheld by man, to a worm like myself, standing as I do, on the very verge of eternity! Another moment, and I cease to exist—and could I find in my bosom room to imagine that the spectators now assembled had forgiven me, the scaffold would have no terrors, nor could the precept which my much respected friend, the marshal of the district, is about to execute. Let me then, in this public manner, return my sincere thanks to him for his kind and gentlemanly deportment during my confinement. He was to me like a father, and his humanity to a dying man I hope will be duly appreciated by an enlightened community.

"My first crime was piracy, for which my life would pay for forfeit on conviction; no punishment could be inflicted on me further than that, and therefore I had nothing to fear but detection, for had my offences been millions of times more aggravated than they are now, death must have satisfied all."

Gibbs having concluded, Wansley began. He said he might be called a pirate, a robber, and a murderer, and he was all of these, but he hoped and trusted God would, through Christ, wash away his aggravated crimes and offences, and not cast him entirely out. His feelings, he said, were so overpowered that he hardly knew how to address those about him, but he frankly admitted the justness of the sentence, and concluded by declaring that he had no hope of pardon except through the atoning blood of his Redeemer, and wished that his sad fate might teach others to shun the broad road to ruin, and travel in that of virtue, which would lead to honor and happiness in this world, and an immortal crown of glory in that to come.

He then shook hands with Gibbs, the officers, and clergy-men—their caps were drawn over their faces, a handkerchief dropped by Gibbs as a signal to the executioner caused the cord to be severed, and in an instant they were suspended in air. Wansley folded his hands before him, soon died with very trifling struggles. Gibbs died hard; before he was run up, and did not again remove them, but after being near two minutes sus-pended, he raised his right hand and partially removed his cap, and in the course of another minute, raised the same hand to his mouth. His dress was a blue round-about jacket and trousers, with a foul anchor in white on his right arm. Wansley wore a white frock coat, trimmed with black, with trousers of the same color.

After the bodies had remained on the gallows the usual time, they were taken down and given to the surgeons for dissection.

# The Real Captain Kidd

### *Frank Stockton*

William Kidd, or Robert Kidd, as he is sometimes called, was a sailor in the merchant service who had a wife and family in New York. He was a very respectable man and had a good reputation as a seaman, and about 1690, when there was war between England and France, Kidd was given the command of a privateer, and having had two or three engagements with French vessels he showed himself to be a brave fighter and a prudent commander.

Some years later he sailed to England, and, while there, he received an appointment of a peculiar character. It was at the time when the King of England was doing his best to put down the pirates of the American coast, and Sir George Bellomont, the recently appointed Governor of New York, recommended Captain Kidd as a very suitable man to command a ship to be sent out to suppress piracy. When Kidd agreed to take the position of chief of marine police, he was not employed by the Crown, but by a small company of gentlemen of capital, who formed themselves into a sort of trust company, or society for the prevention of cruelty to merchantmen, and the object of their association was not only to put down pirates, but to put some money in their own pockets as well.

Kidd was furnished with two commissions, one appointing him a privateer with authority to capture French vessels, and the other empowering him to seize and destroy all pirate ships. Kidd was ordered in his mission to keep a strict account of all booty captured, in order that it might be fairly divided among those who were stockholders in the enterprise, one-tenth of the total proceeds being reserved for the King.

Kidd sailed from England in the *Adventure,* a large ship with thirty guns and eighty men, and on his way to America he captured a French ship, which he carried to New York. Here he arranged to make his crew a great deal larger than had been thought necessary in England, and, by offering a fair share of the property he might confiscate on piratical or French ships, he induced a great many able seamen to enter his service, and when the *Adventure* left New York she carried a crew of one hundred and fifty-five men.

With a fine ship and a strong crew, Kidd now sailed out of the harbor with the ostensible purpose of putting down piracy in American waters, but the methods of this legally appointed marine policeman were very peculiar, and, instead of cruising up and down our coast, he gayly sailed away to the island of Madeira, and then around the Cape of Good Hope to Madagascar and the Red Sea, thus getting himself as far out of his regular beat as any New York constable would have been had he undertaken to patrol the dominions of the Khan of Tartary.

By the time Captain Kidd reached that part of the world he had been at sea for nearly a year without putting down any pirates or capturing any French ships. In fact, he had made no money whatever for himself or the stockholders of the company which had sent him out. His men, of course, must have been very much surprised at this unusual neglect of his own and his employers' interests, but when he reached the Red Sea, he boldly informed them that he had made a change in his business, and had decided that he would be no longer a suppressor of piracy, but would become a pirate himself; and, instead of taking prizes of French ships only—which he was legally empowered to do— he would try to capture any valuable ship he could find on the seas, no matter to what nation it belonged. He then went on to state that his present purpose in coming into those oriental waters was to capture the rich fleet from Mocha which was due in the lower part of the Red Sea about that time.

The crew of the *Adventure,* who must have been tired of having very little to do and making no money, expressed their entire approbation of their captain's change of purpose, and readily agreed to become pirates.

Kidd waited a good while for the Mocha fleet, but it did not arrive, and then he made his first venture in actual piracy. He overhauled a Moorish vessel which was commanded by an English captain, and as England was not at war with Morocco, and as the nationality of the ship's commander should have protected him, Kidd thus boldly broke the marine laws which governed the civilized world and stamped himself an out-and-out pirate. After the exercise of considerable cruelty he extorted from his first prize a small amount of money; and although he and his men did not gain very much booty, they had whetted their appetites for more, and Kidd cruised savagely over the eastern seas in search of other spoils.

After a time the *Adventure* fell in with a fine English ship, called the *Royal Captain,* and although she was probably laden with a rich cargo, Kidd did not attack her. His piratical character was not yet sufficiently formed to give him the disloyal audacity which would enable him, with his English ship and his English crew, to fall upon another English ship manned by another English crew. In time his heart might be hardened, but he felt that he could not begin with this sort of thing just yet. So the *Adventure* saluted the *Royal Captain* with ceremonious politeness, and each vessel passed quietly on its way. But this conscientious consideration did not suit Kidd's crew. They had already had a taste of booty, and they were hungry for more, and when the fine English vessel, of which they might so easily have made a prize, was allowed to escape them, they were loud in their complaints and grumblings.

One of the men, a gunner named William Moore, became actually impertinent upon the subject, and he and Captain Kidd had a violent quarrel, in the course of which the captain picked up a heavy iron-bound bucket and struck the dissatisfied gunner on the head with it. The blow was such a powerful one that the man's skull was broken, and he died the next day.

Captain Kidd's conscience seems to have been a good deal in his way; for although he had been sailing about in various eastern waters, taking prizes wherever he could, he was anxious that reports of his misdeeds should not get home before him.

Having captured a fine vessel bound westward, he took from her all the booty he could, and then proceeded to arrange matters so that the capture of this ship should appear to be a legal transaction. The ship was manned by Moors and commanded by a Dutchman, and of course Kidd had no right to touch it, but the sharp-witted and business-like pirate selected one of the passengers and made him sign a paper declaring that he was a Frenchman, and that he commanded the ship. When this statement had been sworn to before witnesses, Kidd put the document in his pocket so that if he were called upon to explain the transaction he might be able to show that he had good reason to suppose that he had captured a French ship, which, of course, was all right and proper.

Kidd now ravaged the East India waters with great success and profit, and at last he fell in with a very fine ship from Armenia, called the *Quedagh Merchant*, commanded by an Englishman. Kidd's conscience had been growing harder and harder every day, and he did not now hesitate to attack any vessel. The great merchantman was captured, and proved to be one of the most valuable prizes ever taken by a pirate, for Kidd's own share of the spoils amounted to more than sixty thousand dollars. This was such a grand haul that Kidd lost no time in taking his prize to some place where he might safely dispose of her cargo, and get rid of her passengers. Accordingly he sailed for Madagascar. While he was there he fell in with the first pirate vessel he had met since he had started out to put down piracy. This was a ship commanded by an English pirate named Culliford, and here would have been a chance for Captain Kidd to show that, although he might transgress the law himself, he would be true to his engagement not to allow other people to do so; but he had given up putting down piracy, and instead of apprehending Culliford he went into partnership with him, and the two agreed to go pirating together.

This partnership, however, did not continue long, for Captain Kidd began to believe that it was time for him to return to his native country and make a report of his proceedings to his employers. Having confined his piratical proceedings to distant parts of the world, he hoped that he would be able to make Sir George Bellomont and the other stockholders suppose that his booty was all legitimately taken from French vessels cruising in the east, and when the proper division should be made he would be able to quietly enjoy his portion of the treasure he had gained.

He did not go back in the *Adventure,* which was probably not large enough to carry all the booty he had amassed, but putting everything on board his latest prize, the *Quedagh Merchant,* he burned his old ship and sailed homeward.

When he reached the West Indies, however, our wary sea-robber was very much surprised to find that accounts of his evil deeds had reached America, and that the colonial authorities had been so much incensed by the news that the man who had been sent out to suppress piracy had become himself a pirate, that they had circulated notices throughout the different colonies urging the arrest of Kidd if he should come into any American port. This was disheartening intelligence for the treasure-laden Captain Kidd, but he did not despair; he knew that the love of money was often as strong in the minds of human beings as the love of justice. Sir George Bellomont, who was now in New York, was one of the principal stockholders in the enterprise, and Kidd hoped that the rich share of the results of his industry, which would come to the Governor, might cause unpleasant reports to be disregarded. In this case he might yet return to his wife and family with a neat little fortune, and without danger of being called upon to explain his exceptional performances in the eastern seas.

Of course Kidd was not so foolish and rash as to sail into New York harbor on board the *Quedagh Merchant,* so he bought a small sloop and put the most valuable portion of his goods on board her, leaving his larger vessel, which also contained a great quantity of merchandise, in the charge of one of his confederates, and in the little sloop he cautiously approached the coast of New Jersey. His great desire was to find out what sort of a reception he might expect, so he entered Delaware Bay, and when he stopped at a little seaport in order to take in some supplies, he discovered that there was but small chance of his visiting his home and his family, and of making a report to his superior in the character of a deserving mariner who had returned after a successful voyage. Some people in the village recognized him, and the report soon spread to New York that the pirate Kidd was lurking about the coast. A sloop of war was sent out to capture his vessel, and finding that it was impossible to remain in the vicinity where he had been discovered, Kidd sailed northward and entered Long Island Sound.

Here the shrewd and anxious pirate began to act the part of the watch dog who has been killing sheep. In every way he endeavored to assume the appearance of innocence and to conceal every sign of misbehavior. He wrote to Sir George Bellomont that he should have called upon him in order to report his proceedings and hand over his profits, were it not for the wicked and malicious reports which had been circulated about him.

It was during this period of suspense, when the returned pirate did not know what was likely to happen, that it is supposed, by the believers in the hidden treasures of Kidd, that he buried his coin and bullion and his jewels, some in one place and some in another, so that if he were captured his riches would not be taken with him. Among the wild stories which were believed at that time, and for long years after, was one to the effect that Captain Kidd's ship was chased up the Hudson River by a man-of-war, and that the pirates, finding they could not get away, sank their ship and fled to the shore with all the gold and silver they could carry, which they afterwards buried at the foot of Dunderberg Mountain. A great deal of rocky soil has been turned over at different times in search of these treasures, but no discoveries of hidden coin have yet been reported. The fact is, however, that during this time of anxious waiting Kidd never sailed west of Oyster Bay in Long Island. He was afraid to approach New York, although he had frequent communication with that city, and was joined by his wife and family.

About this time occurred an incident which has given rise to all the stories regarding the buried treasure of Captain Kidd. The disturbed and anxious pirate concluded that it was a dangerous thing to keep so much valuable treasure on board his vessel, which might at any time be overhauled by the authorities, and he therefore landed at Gardiner's Island on the Long Island coast, and obtained permission from the proprietor to bury some of his superfluous stores upon his estate. This was a straightforward transaction. Mr. Gardiner knew all about the burial of the treasure, and when it was afterwards proved that Kidd was really a pirate the hidden booty was all given up to the government.

This appears to be the only case in which it was positively known that Kidd buried treasure on our coast, and it has given rise to all the stories of the kind which have ever been told.

For some weeks Kidd's sloop remained in Long Island Sound, and then he took courage and went to Boston to see some influential people there. He was allowed to go freely about the city for a week, and then he was arrested.

The rest of Kidd's story is soon told; he was sent to England for trial, and there he was condemned to death, not only for the piracies he had committed, but also for the murder of William Moore. He was executed, and his body was hung in chains on the banks of the Thames, where for years it dangled in the wind, a warning to all evil-minded sailors.

It is said that Kidd showed no repentance when he was tried, but insisted that he was the victim of malicious persons who swore falsely against him. And yet a more thoroughly dishonest rascal never sailed under the black flag. In the guise of an accredited officer of the government, he committed the crimes he was sent out to suppress; he deceived his men; he robbed and misused his fellow-countrymen and his friends, and he even descended to the meanness of cheating and despoiling the natives of the West India Islands, with whom he traded. These people were in the habit of supplying pirates with food and other necessaries, and they always found their rough customers entirely honest, and willing to pay for what they received; for as the pirates made a practice of stopping at certain points for supplies, they wished, of course, to be on good terms with those who furnished them. But Kidd had no ideas of honor toward people of high or low degree. He would trade with the natives as if he intended to treat them fairly and pay for all he got; but when the time came for him to depart, and he was ready to weigh anchor, he would seize upon all the commodities he could lay his hands upon, and without paying a copper to the distressed and indignant Indians, he would gayly sail away, his black flag flaunting derisively in the wind.

But although in reality Captain Kidd was no hero, he has been known for a century and more as the great American pirate, and his name has been representative of piracy ever since. Years after he had been hung, when people heard that a vessel with a black flag, or one which looked black in the distance, flying from its rigging had been seen, they forgot that the famous pirate was dead, and imagined that Captain Kidd was visiting their part of the coast in order that he might find a good place to bury some treasure which it was no longer safe for him to carry about.

There were two great reasons for the fame of Captain Kidd. One of these was the fact that he had been sent out by important officers of the crown who expected to share the profits of his legitimate operations, but who were supposed by their enemies to be perfectly willing to take any sort of profits provided it could not be proved that they were the results of piracy, and who afterwards allowed Kidd to suffer for their sins as well as his own. These opinions introduced certain political features into his career and made him a very much talked-of man. The greater reason for his fame, however, was the widespread belief in his buried treasures, and this made him the object of the most intense interest to hundreds of misguided people who hoped to be lucky enough to share his spoils.

There were other pirates on the American coast during the eighteenth century, and some of them became very well known, but their stories are not uncommon, and we need not tell them here. As our country became better settled, and as well-armed revenue cutters began to cruise up and down our Atlantic coast for the protection of our commerce, pirates became fewer and fewer, and even those who were still bold enough to ply their trade grew milder in their manners, less daring in their exploits, and—more important than anything else—so unsuccessful in their illegal enterprises that they were forced to admit that it was now more profitable to command or work a merchantman than endeavor to capture one, and so the sea-robbers of our coasts gradually passed away.

# Sources

"The Pirates Code," from *The Pirate's Who's Who*, 1924

"Blackbeard in Virginia," from *The Story of Jack Ballister's Fortunes*, 1894

"The Terrible Ladrones," from *Great Pirate Stories*, 1922

"The Malay Proas," from *Afloat and Ashore: A Sea Tale*, 1844

"The Granddaughter of the Great Mogul," from *The King of Pirates*, 1719

"The Man with the Belt of Gold," from *Kidnapped*, 1886

"Captain Sharkey," from *Tales of Pirates and Blue Water*, 1922

"A Thief and a Pirate," from *Captain Blood*, 1922

"A Lady among the Pirates," translated by Amelia B. Edwards from *A Lady's Captivity among Chinese Pirates in the Chinese Seas*, circa 1860

"Pieces of Eight," from *Treasure Island*, 1883

"The Atrocious Life of Charles Gibbs," from *The Pirate's Own Book*, 1837

"The Real Captain Kidd," from *Buccaneers and Pirates of Our Coasts*, 1898